That's When He Made His Mistake. Before She Could Escape, He Reached Out And Caught Her Hand In His.

It hit with all the heat and power of a lightning bolt, stunning him. The sizzle, the inner sparks, the arc of want and desire, like someone had forced his entire body into a light socket and then amped up the juice. It all cascaded through him in an unending torrent. It wasn't that it hurt, it just surprised him. Worse, it horrified him because he had a hideous feeling he knew what caused it. He'd heard the stories over the years. Watched as one by one, cousin and brother had fallen to its insidious influence.

Shayla pulled back from him. "What was that?" she demanded, her brows snapping together. "What did you just do to me?"

"Son of a—" He shook his head to clear it. "I think I just Infernoed you."

Dear Reader,

One of the fun parts of writing stories about the Dantes—stories that stand alone or can be enjoyed as part of the whole—is building family relationships. I love the various roles each member plays, mainly because I come from a large family. I've always been fascinated by the interaction and dynamics that result when such different and individual people are thrown into the same mixing bowl. Often times, it's chaos!

For instance, one family member is known as Queen of the Universe. Another as The Rebel. Still another as Mr. Organization. During my teen years, my brother dubbed me The Girl Who Lives Upstairs because I liked to hide out in my room and read and write. I think that's what has made the Dantes such a joy is that I can explore each aspect of these very different men and women and uncover their unique role in the family.

This story, *Dante's Marriage Pact,* starts at the very same glittering affair as the last book, *Dante's Temporary Fiancée.* It's a Dante reception that doesn't ignite just one Inferno match, but two. Read on to discover how Draco, the troublemaker of the group, learns the true meaning of trouble when a one-night stand turns into something far deeper and more lasting. And I hope you notice the small Dante bombshell that's dropped in the last chapter!

All the best,

Day Leclaire

DAY LECLAIRE

DANTE'S
MARRIAGE PACT

Silhouette Desire

Published by Silhouette Books
America's Publisher of Contemporary Romance

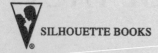 SILHOUETTE BOOKS

ISBN-13: 978-0-373-73070-4

Recycling programs
for this product may
not exist in your area.

DANTE'S MARRIAGE PACT

Copyright © 2010 by Day Totton Smith

This edition published by arrangement with Harlequin Books S.A.

For questions and comments about the quality of this book please contact us
at Customer_eCare@Harlequin.ca.

® and TM are trademarks of Harlequin Books S.A., used under license.
Trademarks indicated with ® are registered in the United States Patent
and Trademark Office, the Canadian Trade Marks Office and in other
countries.

Visit Silhouette Books at www.eHarlequin.com

Printed in U.S.A.

Books by Day Leclaire

Silhouette Desire

*The Forbidden Princess #1780
*The Prince's Mistress #1786
*The Royal Wedding Night #1792
The Billionaire's Baby
   Negotiation #1821
†Dante's Blackmailed Bride #1852
   (Severo & Francesca's story)
†Dante's Stolen Wife #1870
   (Marco & Caitlyn's story)
†Dante's Wedding Deception #1880
   (Nicolò & Kiley's story)
†Dante's Contract Marriage #1899
   (Lazzaro & Ariana's story)

Mr. Strictly Business #1921
Inherited: One Child #1953
Lone Star Seduction #1983
†Dante's Ultimate Gamble #2017
   (Luciano and Téa's story)
†Dante's Temporary Fiancée #2037
   (Rafaelo and Larkin's story)
†Dante's Marriage Pact #2057
   (Draco and Shayla's story)

*The Royals
†The Dante Legacy

DAY LECLAIRE

USA TODAY bestselling author Day Leclaire is described by Harlequin Books as "one of our most popular writers ever!" Day's tremendous worldwide popularity has made her a member of Harlequin's "Five Star Club," with sales of well over five million books. She is a three-time winner of both a Colorado Award of Excellence and a Golden Quill Award. She's won *RT Book Reviews* Career Achievement and Love and Laughter Awards, a Holt Medallion and a Booksellers' Best Award. She has also received an impressive ten nominations for the prestigious Romance Writers of America's RITA® Award.

Day's romances touch the heart and make you care about her characters as much as she does. In Day's own words, "I adore writing romances, and can't think of a better way to spend each day." For more information, visit Day on her website, www.dayleclaire.com.

To Carolyn Greene,
who holds my hand through the best and the worst.

One

She was a nervous wreck.

Shayla Charleston stood in the luxurious bathroom at the San Francisco headquarters of Dantes, one of the world's premier jewelry empires, and regarded herself in the mirror. To her relief her nerves didn't show, and once she got through tonight this would all be over. Not only that, but tomorrow she'd turn twenty-five and maybe, just maybe, fulfill each of the three goals she had set for herself.

Goal number one: Pay back her grandmother. Shayla had worked like a dog these past three years to reimburse Grandmother Charleston for the cost of her college education, an education her grandmother had scrimped and saved for, even at the risk of allowing their home to decay around their ears. Though her grandmother had hoped Shayla would resurrect the family business, she hadn't inherited the talent or the ability. But she could and would represent the family interests when she met with members of the

Dante clan tomorrow. If she were very lucky, that meeting would provide her grandmother with badly needed financial security, something Shayla would do anything to ensure, no matter how difficult.

Goal number two: Get the job of her dreams. Shayla smiled broadly. Check, check and double check. The minute she escaped her meeting with the Dantes, she'd climb on a plane headed straight for Europe, where she'd begin her job as a translator for the highly reclusive international businessman, Derek Algier. The job would take her to some of the most beautiful and exotic countries in the world and she flat-out could not wait.

Goal number three: Tomorrow, before she assumed her new responsibilities, Shayla wanted to be swept off her feet and experience a mad, impetuous romance. Just this once. One night of passion before she reverted to her more reserved, dependable nature. Was that too much to ask?

She pressed an anxious hand to her stomach. But first, she had a party to crash.

The door to the restroom opened and several women entered. Everyone exchanged polite smiles and one of the women gave Shayla's gown an envious glance. It relieved her mind since it confirmed that the alterations she'd made to her mother's designer gown—one left over from the Charlestons' glory days—were invisible to even the most discerning eye.

Even better, a quick, assessing glance in the mirror assured her that her makeup looked exactly right, as did her hair. Considering the lighting conditions and scratched mirror in the cheap little motel room she'd rented, all she could afford at this point, it was a miracle that she'd managed to pull it together as well as she had. No question about it, she exuded wealth and privilege, something the Charlestons hadn't experienced in a full decade thanks to the Dantes.

Now to do a little reconnaissance in anticipation of tomorrow's meeting. If she could get a feel for some of the prime players, she just might gain an edge in their negotiations, something she badly needed considering how out of her depth she was. She reached for her vintage beaded handbag and the list buried inside, dismayed to discover that the clasp had once again popped open when she'd set it on the counter.

The bag had also been her mother's, another echo from the past that whispered of genteel elegance and casual prosperity. She wouldn't have minded the broken clasp except for one not-so-minor detail.

The items she carried inside were worth millions.

She couldn't afford to lose the precious bundle. Unlike her college education, she'd never be able to repay her grandmother for the loss. Reaching inside, Shayla tucked the leather pouch into the deepest corner of the bag—not that it was terribly deep. Then she extracted the list her grandmother had given her and scanned the names one last time, committing them to memory.

Primo Dante, the family patriarch and founder of the Dantes jewelry empire, now retired. Severo Dante, CEO and chairman of the board. Then there were the twins. Marco handled international sales and relations. She doubted she'd meet him. Lazzaro was their chief financial officer. Guaranteed he'd sit in on the meeting. That was the best intel her grandmother had to offer and that her own research could turn up, which would have to do.

Satisfied that she had the names down pat, Shayla refolded the paper and tucked it into her handbag. She double-checked to make certain she secured the clasp good and tight. Taking a deep breath, she examined her appearance one final time and nodded. She could only hope she'd fit in.

Exiting the restroom, she scanned the guests waiting in the foyer outside of the reception. This would be the most difficult part, and most traumatic for someone of her nature. Security stood at the doorway collecting invitations. She waited until a large, laughing crowd descended and attached herself to one side, slipping past during the momentary confusion. And just like that, she crashed the Dantes' reception. She hastened across the threshold and focused. First business. Check out the Dantes on her list.

Then maybe she'd find the perfect man, a man who'd make tonight the most special of her life.

Draco Dante noticed her the instant she stepped into the room. Noticed her, and wanted her with a fierceness that nearly brought him to his knees. He felt the visceral tug of attraction and didn't resist. Of course, at that point he didn't fully appreciate the ramifications of what was happening. Or if he did, he assumed on some level that he could fight free from its hold whenever he wanted. He didn't realize The Inferno had set its hooks in him and was reeling him toward his doom. He still believed himself in control of his own destiny.

Until that night he'd never believed in The Inferno. Never believed in the family legend—or curse, as some considered it. In his opinion it was ludicrous to think that a man could identify his soul mate with a simple touch. Ridiculous to believe that there even were such things as soul mates. Resisted with all his might the possibility that there was one woman out there meant just for him…and only one. He'd heard the stories over the years. Watched as one by one, cousin and brother had fallen to its insidious influence. But whatever this was, whatever hit him when he first set eyes on this woman stole every thought from his head save one.

Take the woman.

At a guess she stood a full five foot eight and had a wealth of hair knotted at her nape, the ebony color a perfect complement to her ink-blotch eyes. Though her curves weren't voluptuous they were impressive enough to capture the attention of most of the men in the room. Or maybe it was the way she displayed them, in a ruby-red halter dress that hugged her breasts and nipped in at her narrow waist before pouring over shapely hips and a deliciously rounded backside.

She stepped across the threshold and moved with graceful purpose toward a corner display out of the main flow of traffic.

He headed toward her, cutting off the competition with a neat sidestep. She stood in front of one of the Eternity wedding band displays, riveted by the rings, her full attention focused on them. "Beautiful, aren't they?" he said.

She continued to study the display, effectively ignoring him. "Stunning," she murmured.

"I believe this is the part where we're supposed to introduce ourselves," he prompted with a smile.

"No, thanks," she said with a quick, reserved glance and shifted to move around him.

That's when he made his mistake. Before she could escape, he reached out and caught her hand in his. "Wait—"

It hit with all the heat and power of a lightning bolt, stunning him. The sizzle, the inner sparks, the arc of want and desire, like someone had forced his entire body into a light socket and then amped up the juice. It all cascaded through him in an unending torrent. It wasn't that it hurt, it just surprised him. Worse, it horrified him because he had a hideous feeling he'd just confirmed his worst suspicions.

She pulled back from him. "What was that?" she demanded, her brows snapping together. "What did you just do to me?"

"Son of a—" He shook his head to clear it. "I think I just Infernoed you."

"Well, don't do it again. I didn't like it." With that, she turned her back on him and disappeared into the crowd.

It took Draco an instant to react. Not certain whether to swear or laugh—maybe both—he went after the woman. He caught up with her near another display.

He stood at her side, not that she took any notice. "Are you telling me that you only felt a shock when we touched? It wasn't anything more than that?"

Her attention remained fixed on the gems as though they held the answer to all of life's mysteries. "Was I supposed to feel something more?"

"The way I've heard it…yes."

She turned her head and regarded him with a curious stare. Her eyes were large and tilted at the edges, and filled with something sad and ageless. They were also stunning in their ability to convey her every emotion. And right now they conveyed a clear message: Go. Away. "I have no idea what you're talking about."

Why was it that the one woman he wanted more than any other wouldn't give him the time of day? If it weren't so frustrating, it would be funny. "Maybe we could start over. I'm—"

She whirled to confront him, the skirt of her dress flaring around her, the hem catching at his legs as though eager to embrace him. She pressed her fingertips to his lips. "No names," she whispered urgently. "I'm crashing the party and if I get caught, you can honestly say you don't know who I am. That way you won't get into trouble, too."

Aw, hell. He didn't dare admit he was a Dante now. "Are you here to steal something?"

Astonishment mingled with shock. No way could she have faked that look. "No, of course not."

"That's good." Very good. "How about first names? People do exchange them, you know, even when they're crashing parties." Because of his position as Dantes' head gemologist, he was extremely careful to keep his rather unusual name out of the spotlight, so she shouldn't connect it with the Dante family.

She caught her lower lip between her teeth and the top of his head almost came off. More than anything he wanted that sweet, succulent lip captured between his own teeth. "I guess that can't hurt," she conceded. "I'm Shayla."

"Draco," he said. "Draco-with-no-last-name."

"Oh, dear." She offered a teasing smile. "Did your parents dislike you?"

"What, Draco?" He returned her smile with a rueful one of his own. "It's a family name. My mother's maiden name. I also had it long before *Harry Potter* came out, in case you were wondering."

"It means dragon, doesn't it?"

"Afraid so."

A hint of hesitation flowed across her expression. "And are you?"

"A dragon?" He pondered the idea. "I can be when it's important to me. If someone takes what I consider mine."

"Then I'll have to make sure I avoid taking anything you value."

"Always a wise move."

He decided to experiment and shifted closer to see how Shayla would respond. Her reaction was so subtle, he almost missed it. But it was there. It was definitely there. The thick fringe of her eyelashes flickered ever so slightly and tension swept across her shoulders. It didn't make sense to him. Why hide it? If it were anything similar to what he felt right this minute, she should be falling all over him.

The Inferno—assuming it really was The Inferno, and he still had his doubts about that—clouded rational thought, driving a man to find a way to touch the woman he craved, to inhale her. To carry her off and bury himself in her until neither of them could move or think or breathe.

"Why are you fighting it?" he asked in an undertone.

"Fighting what?"

This time she couldn't hide the lie and he didn't waste time arguing. Before she realized his intention, he caught her hand in his. Heat flared between them, more intense this time, pouring into his veins like effervescent champagne. Every beat of his heart drove it further and deeper, strengthening the connection until it threatened to overpower him.

"Shayla..."

He whispered her name into the few inches of space separating them, filling the sound with every ounce of the desire he felt. Her lips parted and her breathing quickened. She swayed, yielding ever so slightly. He caught the subtle fragrance of her perfume, crisp and spicy with a dash of sultry thrown in. Somehow he suspected the scent epitomized the woman.

"What have you done to me?"

She asked the question with such bewilderment that he flinched. "I'm sorry. It isn't something I can control."

"I don't have time for this right now. Make it stop."

Draco didn't insult her with prevarication. "I wouldn't even if I could. I want you, sweetheart. And I think you want me, too."

She closed her eyes and he wondered if she were fighting the tug, that relentless, unyielding pull. Not that she could win this particular battle. At least... No one ever had. "I have something else I need to take care of first," she whispered.

He moved in, erasing those few inches that separated them, just close enough so hips and thighs brushed. Just enough so he felt the soft crush of her breasts against his chest. Just enough so his mouth hovered within a whisper of her lips. "Whatever you're here for can wait. This can't."

She looked at him, enchanting him with an open display of pleasure and desire. She utterly captivated him. She was swift to smile, swifter to laugh, her movements like quicksilver, filled with energy, yet as graceful as a dancer's. He wanted all that grace and energy in his bed. Wanted that magical sparkle for himself. Like a dragon hoarding his treasure, came the whimsical thought. "I've never done this before. Never lost control or acted so impulsively," she admitted.

"I'm wish I could say the same. Tell me you're not going to fight what we're feeling."

Her mouth quivered on the verge of a smile. "I'm not sure I could."

He bent his head and feathered a kiss along her jawline. "That makes two of us. So, instead of crashing this very boring party, why don't you sneak away with me? I promise I won't bore you."

She shuddered in reaction. Then her smile blossomed and the soft sound of her laughter made it clear that whatever connection they'd forged during these brief moments together had won out. The day had already been an interesting one. First, he'd received a phone call from his brother's ex-investigator, Juice, with news that another fire diamond had been found...the fourth of six that had been stolen from Draco in a clever swindle a full decade before. This new information gave him one more opportunity to find the person behind the con.

And now the most beautiful woman Draco had ever seen had walked into the reception and blew his earlier convictions about The Inferno straight out of the water. Or, maybe it wasn't The Inferno. Maybe it was just a bad case of lust or a sexual lightning bolt of some kind.

"What is this?" she asked. Her voice, though low, carried a wealth of passion flavored with a sweet Southern warmth. Georgia? Or perhaps South Carolina. "And why you and not some other man here?" She gestured to indicate the milling crowd. "I don't understand what's happening."

The thought of Shayla giving herself to someone else filled Draco with a ferocity that he could barely wrestle into submission. "I don't know how or why we formed this connection," he admitted. "Not exactly. But if it makes you feel any better, it's the same for me."

He couldn't resist. He had to touch her. He skimmed the tips of his fingers along the inside of her forearm from elbow to wrist in a silent demand. *Come with me.* It was like touching a silken thread of fire. She shivered in response and swayed toward him, giving him an equally silent answer. Sliding his arm around her waist, he drew her through the doorway of the reception area and down a long corridor toward a bank of private elevators. He used his key to access the car and the minute the doors parted, they stepped inside. He inserted his key again to access the top floor, which housed four private penthouse suites.

She frowned when she realized which button he'd pushed. "Where are we going?"

"Up." The single-word answer didn't satisfy her, but right now it took every ounce of focus and determination to keep his hands off her.

"And what is up there?"

"Dantes maintains suites for visiting clients from out of town who are anxious to exchange their millions for one of Dantes' premier collections. I'm staying in one temporarily." For some reason the information caused her to relax ever so slightly. "It also gives us a place where we can discuss our situation without the risk of interruption."

"Just discuss?"

He gave it to her straight. "That depends."

She tilted her head to one side. "On what?"

"On what we want to do about this." He took her hand in his, lacing their fingers together in order to make his point.

She drew in a sharp breath, her dark eyes flaming with desire. "What is that?" she asked unevenly. "And this time I expect an answer. A straight answer, if you don't mind."

Fortunately, the doors parted before he had to try to put it into words. The instant they stepped off the elevator, he tugged at her hand, drawing her across the foyer to a door leading to his penthouse suite. His stay there was a temporary situation during the planning and building stages of his new home. Only one of the other three suites was currently occupied, housing the King and Queen of Verdonia, rulers of the country that supplied Dantes with the most beautiful amethysts in the world. Many of the Eternity rings on display this evening featured their gemstones.

Fumbling with his keys, Draco found the correct one. He shoved it into the lock, and managed to get the door open and the appropriate alarm code entered before sweeping her into his arms and carrying her across the threshold. He didn't bother to analyze the symbolism of his actions. His main concern was to lock the two of them away while he coaxed her into the nearest bed. Assuming he lasted long enough to find his bed.

He carried her through to the expansive living room, one that offered views of both the city and the bay. Setting her on her feet, he took her clutch purse and tossed it in the general direction of the couch. It bounced on the cushion and then somersaulted onto the floor.

She started in alarm. "No, wait. My purse—"

"—will be there in the morning."

He reached for her, but she held up a hand before he could pull her back into his arms. She shot an uneasy glance in the direction her purse had taken. She must have decided it was safe enough for the time being because she returned her focus to him.

"Just wait a moment, Draco." He loved the way her voice caressed his name, drawing it out and layering a soft Southern hitch onto the two syllables. "You said you would explain what caused that spark when we first touched. Before this goes any further, I want to know how you did that."

"I'm sorry if I hurt you." He spoke with utter sincerity. "It wasn't deliberate."

She stared at her hand, rubbing her palm with her thumb, before eyeing him warily. "It hasn't gone away."

"It will." He hoped.

She lifted an eyebrow. "And what, exactly, is *it?*"

"Our family calls it The Inferno," he reluctantly admitted, deliberately not using his last name in case it scared her off. "When we're intensely attracted to certain women, it causes that sort of reaction."

"Certain women?" She wavered between outrage and curiosity. "What do you mean by that?"

He hesitated, aware that a deep pit yawned in front of him. He chose his words with care, hoping they'd help him skirt disaster. "Women we want. Women we're intensely attracted to. At least, I'm assuming that's what generated the sparks between us. To be honest, it's never happened to me before."

"Got it." Her mouth twitched. "It's your version of a mating call."

It was his turn to feel a flash of outrage, though it was edged with amusement. "Hell, at least I'm not bugling and pawing the ground," he muttered.

"You just roar and breathe fire?" she suggested with a teasing laugh.

"Only with you." If the words contained a growling hint

of that roar, there was nothing he could do to prevent it. She'd just have to be grateful he didn't spew flames.

He waited. All the while the want flared higher and stronger than ever before. She was right. If he could roar and breathe fire, he'd do it. Hell, if it meant winning her for his mate, he'd sprout wings and carry her off to the nearest lair, assuming such a thing existed.

He saw her soften and realized he'd avoided the trap. Better yet, she came into his arms as though she belonged, which on some level she did. Maybe on every level.

It was his last rational thought for a long time.

He cupped her face and then paused to appreciate the moment. Her lips parted in anticipation, damp and full, while desire openly shaped her expression. No pretense. No hesitation. Just pure passion freely offered. She was beyond lovely. And yet, even as he studied her, a hint of bewilderment filled her eyes with a sooty darkness.

"Are you having second thoughts?" she asked.

"Not a single one."

"Oh." Her expression revealed a heart-wrenching vulnerability. "I thought you were going to kiss me now that we have that Inferno problem out of the way. But you haven't."

"Ah, but this is a first kiss."

She considered his words. "And that makes a difference?"

"It makes a huge difference." He continued to scrutinize her face. "A first kiss… You remember that one. It makes an indelible impression. It deserves the proper amount of thought and consideration. For instance, are you the sort of woman who likes a slow, leisurely exploration? Should I sample your mouth the way I would taste a new dish, in small cautious bites?"

"That's a definite possibility," she agreed.

He tilted his head to one side and shook his head. "But

not quite right for you. Maybe this hunger between us needs to be fed fast. Attacked. Wrestled into submission with hard, explosive kisses."

The breath shivered from her lungs. "Tempting…" The word escaped on a sigh of longing.

"More tempting than you can imagine," he admitted. "But still not right for a first kiss. Hard and fast will come later."

A hint of amusement mingled with her longing. "But it will come?"

"Without question."

"And for our first kiss?" A thread of urgency spun through her question.

"Kissing you will be like sampling a rare wine." He leaned in, so close their lips almost touched. "First, there's the appearance. The color and sparkle. The deep, rich ebony of your eyes. The way they glitter against your pale skin." He swept his thumbs across her cheeks. "The hint of roses." His breath caressed her lips. "The blaze of rubies."

"Funny. I see emeralds and gold." Her smile blossomed, filled with enchantment. "And just a hint of amber."

Is that how his eyes appeared to her? He lowered his head to the silken joining of shoulder and throat, warming it with his breath. "And next comes the scent, that delicious bouquet of flower and fruit and spice that floods the senses and drives the anticipation. And you do, sweetheart. You flood my senses."

Her eyes fluttered closed as she breathed him in. "You smell like a forest, cedar mixed with an undertone of something earthy and highly masculine."

His body clenched at the undisguised need rippling through her comment. "Do you like it?"

"Very much." The words sighed from her, making it almost impossible to continue.

All he wanted was to take her—here and now—but he

fought the urge, fought to seduce her inch by agonizing inch. "And then there's that first taste," he managed to say. He brushed his lips across hers, just the lightest of touches before drawing back. "A mere sample, to tease and delight."

She followed where he led, lifting toward him, trembling in her urgency. "Taste me again, Draco. Now."

This time he didn't resist. He took her mouth, the taking firm and thorough, revealing a hint of the intense desire that drove him to the brink of insanity. She tasted sweet, honey-sweet and warm, her hunger a perfect mirror of his own. Her lips were plump and soft and giving. And her skin... Heaven help him, he'd never touched anything so soft.

He cupped her shoulders, bared by the halter top, and tripped his fingertips along her collarbones. She shivered, her mouth parting on a moan. It was a clear offer to deepen the kiss, and he did just that, giving her a hint of hard and explosive. She returned his kiss with a passion he'd only suspected—and hoped—she possessed.

Her arms wrapped around his neck and she threaded her fingers through his hair, tugging him closer so she could give back with an intensity that practically brought him to his knees. The scent of her twined around him, while her mouth tempted and tantalized, dipping inward in brief enticing forays. He let her take the lead. For now. He wanted her to familiarize herself with him—his scent, his taste, his touch.

His possession.

Long minutes slid by while she satisfied that first wave of desire. Then she pulled back just enough to draw in a deep breath. She stared up at him and shook her head in disbelief. "I don't understand any of this. I've never done this before. I mean *never*."

"In that case, I appreciate being the first."

"I'm glad I chose you." Her expression turned impish.

"After all, how often will I have a chance to sample such an excellent vintage?"

She made the comment with such grace and humor that it utterly endeared her to him. She returned to his arms and the quality of their embrace changed, this time becoming more certain in the melding of male to female. More familiar with how their mouths fit together and how their bodies moved one against the other.

But it still wasn't enough. It wouldn't be enough until he had her in his bed, with nothing between them but hot, willing flesh, their bodies joined as man was meant to be joined with his woman.

And in that moment Draco knew. Knew beyond a shadow of a doubt.

Shayla was his Inferno mate.

Two

Draco cupped Shayla's face, tilting it so he could enhance their kiss, sliding from passionate to tender, from tender to demanding, from demanding to teasing. Her heart hammered in time with his own and he absorbed the helpless shudder she gave. His hands shifted, dropping from her face and circling her neck to the clasp hidden beneath the intricate knot of her hair. A quick flick of his fingers released it and the silk poured from her shoulders, baring her breasts.

For a split second his heart and lungs forgot how to function. Never before had he seen such perfection. Slowly he reached for her, drawing out the moment until it was bowstring-taut. Gently, oh, so gently, he sculpted her with his fingertips. She trembled in reaction and her nipples pearled into tight, deep rosy peaks.

"Draco..." His name shuddered in the air, filled with a bittersweet yearning. "Please."

"Don't ask me to rush this." He barely recognized the

low, gruff tenor of his voice, filled with dark hunger. "I can't. I won't. I want it to be perfect, not some fast, awkward tumble."

A smile flirted with her mouth, a mouth still full and red from his kisses. "Just out of curiosity, are you even capable of a fast, awkward tumble?"

"I hope not." Dear heaven, he hoped not. "But everything about you makes me lose control."

Her smile grew. "Everything?"

He leaned in and inhaled her unique perfume. "Your scent." He circled the areola of her nipple with his index finger. "The silky feel of your skin. Your taste…"

He drew the tip of her breast into his mouth, nipping at the sensitive bud. Her breath caught. Held. Released on a cry of urgent demand. It was an irresistible siren's call.

He had only a vague memory of their transition from the living room to the bedroom. Leaving the lights off, he touched a panel just inside the doorway that activated the window treatments. They opened with a soft swish, silvering the room with starlight and brightening it with the hint of a rising moon.

He eased back, allowing the cool air to momentarily relieve the relentless burn of their passion and enable him to regain some modicum of control. When it came to the current situation, he needed every ounce of that control. He ripped his bow tie from around his neck and, one by one, removed the studs from his shirt front and cuffs. All the while Shayla stood swallowed in shadows, watching his every move with a gaze almost impossible to read.

He tossed his shirt aside and approached. The moonlight brought an unworldly sheen to her skin. She made a stunning palette of soft pearl and glittering jet misted with silver. Only her lips and the gown that clung to her hips added any color, a deep, dense ruby. He considered himself somewhat of a connoisseur of beauty, perhaps because of his occupation. When it came to gemstones, he was an expert—on their grading, their purity, their color and value. And yet, he didn't think he'd ever seen anything or anyone more beautiful than this woman.

She waited for him, unmoving, allowing his touch. Allowing him to slowly lower the zip of her gown. It pooled at her feet and he lifted her free of it.

"We're going to make love now, aren't we?" she asked.

"Yes."

"Will it be like our first kiss?"

He couldn't help smiling. "Better, I hope."

She flashed him a sparkling look, filled with feminine mystery and earthy desire. "Prove it," she whispered.

He lifted an eyebrow. "A challenge?"

"Are you up to it?" Shayla teased.

Oh, hell, yes. "Ask me that again in an hour, though I suspect you'll know the answer yourself by then."

He reached for her, but instead of touching her, he plucked one of the clips from her hair. The heavy mass loosened, edging downward toward her shoulders. He removed the next two and her hair uncoiled, cascading like an ebony waterfall over her shoulders and down her back. He fisted his hand in the strands, surprised by the thickness and weight of it. It seemed too much for her slender neck to bear. And yet, she did.

Gently, he tipped her back onto the bed. She lifted her leg and braced her high-heeled shoe against his abdomen. The tip of her stiletto scraped across the sensitive skin. "Do you mind?"

"Careful," he warned. "You wouldn't want to cut our evening short."

She laughed, soft and low. "No, I wouldn't want that."

He slid her shoe from her foot before lifting her other leg

and repeating the process. Her stockings followed. Finally, he eased away the remaining few scraps of silk and lace, baring her to his gaze. She epitomized everything he'd heard about women from the South. She was all velvet softness and stunning feminine curves. But beneath he could see the shapely sweep of well-toned muscle and sinew. Strength concealed beneath silk. Did the dichotomy also represent the true nature of the woman?

His own clothing followed the same path as hers, and then he was beside her, drawing her into his arms. She slid beneath him and wrapped herself around him. Draco could feel the hammer of her heart against his, hear the hitch of her breath and feel the flush that seemed to flow from her very core. He cupped her, cupped the quickening warmth, and slowly stoked the fire until it threatened to consume them both.

"Draco," she cried, surging toward him, opening to him, nearly sending him straight over the edge.

"I'm right here, sweetheart. Hang on a moment longer." He protected himself before settling between her thighs and moistening himself in her heat. "I don't think I can wait. Fast and furious this first time. Slow and teasing next."

She stiffened ever so slightly. "Maybe we should go with slow this first time. Very slow."

A short, hard laugh exploded from him. "Not sure that's possible."

She held him off with a delicate hand that possessed surprising strength. "You don't understand. Earlier when I said I'd never done this before, I meant that I've never done *any* of this before. If you'd be so kind, I'd really prefer slow until I get the hang of this."

He froze. "You're a virgin?"

She smiled, that enchanting smile that seemed to befuddle every thought in his head. "Not for much longer."

Draco fought for control. Fought to pull away. Fought to

shoehorn honor ahead of desire. He lifted onto his forearms. "Why?" he groaned. "Why me?"

Humor flashed through her dark gaze. "How could I not?" She gathered up his hand, laced it with her fingers so their palms joined. "When you seduced me with one touch."

His amusement matched hers. "*I* seduced *you?* I'm beginning to think it was the other way around." The last few seconds of conversation had helped him regain his control enough to ask one final question, at the very least to slow things down. "Are you sure?"

She pulled him back into her arms, looping her arms around his neck. "Positive."

"But no pressure, right?"

Her soft laugh arrowed through him, leaving him teetering on a knife-sharp precipice. "None."

"I'm relieved to hear it."

No matter what it took, he'd make this night one of the most special of her life. He drew out the preliminaries, stroking the softness of her breasts and belly. Tracing leisurely circles from her toes to her upper thighs. Sketching kisses from hip to hip before tenderly finding the heart of her. Urging her up and up and up until she hovered just within reach of the peak.

Satisfied that her pleasure was at its highest point, he carefully mated his body to hers, easing into her. Teasing and tempting as he penetrated. Moving. Then thrusting. Finally, driving. Edging her closer and closer to that tantalizing moment of climax. She matched his rhythm like a woman born to the dance. Her skin acquired a pearlescent sheen, flushed with passion. And when she gazed up at him, her eyes were ocean-deep, midnight-black and filled with the wonder of newfound desire.

He watched her climb, watched her climax knot the muscles of her body and burn in her eyes. Heard the pleasure of it ripped from her throat as she bowed backward, helpless beneath the onslaught. And he followed her over, one with her in the ultimate melding of male to female. Never had it been like this with any other woman. And he knew—knew beyond doubt and to the very core—that it never would be again. Only with this woman would he experience a bond that took him to such heights.

The aftermath hit and they collapsed into each other's arms. A long moment passed where neither of them had the breath or energy to speak, a moment out of time. A moment where, as a Dante, Draco recognized the power of The Inferno and surrendered to it.

He didn't understand how it had happened or why, but this woman was his soul mate, their destinies woven together in a tapestry just beginning. He had no idea what shape the final picture would take, only that they were bound together from this time forward. He couldn't help but wonder how Shayla would react when she discovered the extent of their bond.

Gently, he rolled to one side and tucked her close. One thing he knew for certain, it would take time to claim this woman. She was quicksilver, impossible to pin down, held only through desire and temptation. She would have to come to him, be coaxed into his arms, his bed and his life through patience—not something he excelled at. But win her he would and before she knew it she'd wake up with a ring on her finger and a husband at her side.

He thought they slept for a short time because when he moved again it felt as though the night had deepened. With a groan, he levered onto an elbow and forked his fingers into her hair. She blinked sleepily at him, her smile filled with sweet delight.

"Hello, there," she murmured.

"I believe you had a question a while ago," he said in a

low, husky voice. "Something about whether our lovemaking would be as good as our kisses. Care to offer an opinion?"

"That's right. I did wonder about that." She wrinkled her brow, pretending to give it serious consideration. "Your kisses are definitely superb. I had serious doubts that anything could surpass them."

"Well, hell," he grumbled. "Now you have me worried."

"As for your lovemaking…"

"Seriously worried."

"…and taking into consideration that I don't have a basis for comparison…"

"Duly noted."

Her teasing expression faded, replaced by a satisfaction he couldn't mistake. "It was beyond imagination, Draco." Remnants of their shared passion underscored her comment. "I never realized it could be so wonderful."

He kissed the tip of her nose. "So you admit that we Dantes—or at least this Dante—is talented in more arenas than just the jewelry business?"

The instant the question left his mouth she stiffened beneath him, staring in shocked disbelief. "*What* did you say?" The question came out low and furious and filled with feminine outrage.

He froze. "What's wrong?" Because, clearly, something was. It must have been something he said. It sure as hell couldn't have been anything he'd done. That had been as close to perfection as he'd ever experienced. "Shayla?"

Her breathing came swift and shallow, almost panicked. "You never told me your last name. Remember, we agreed? When we first met, you just said Draco."

He stared blankly. "What does that matter now? We're not at the reception and I promise I won't tell the rest of my relatives that you crashed the party."

She shoved at his chest. "But you're a Dante."

He kept her pinned in place, determined to have this out, suspecting she'd run if he let her go. "I brought you up here in a private elevator. I used a key, for crying out loud. Who the hell would have access to this floor and this suite if not a Dante?"

"You told me the apartments were reserved for clients. I assumed you were a client of the Dantes." She thumped his chest with her fist. He reluctantly shifted back. The instant he did she squirmed out from beneath him and snatched the sheet against her chest, putting as much distance between them as the bed allowed. "So, it's true? You...you're a *Dante?*"

He glared at her, offended. "You say that as though it were a dirty word. What the hell's wrong with being a Dante?"

Shayla scooped up the wings of her hair and hooked them behind her ears. How could this have happened? How could she not have realized? The one time, the very first time, she allowed passion to override common sense *this* happened. She'd given her virginity to the one man she should have avoided at all costs, whose family had destroyed her own and left them utterly destitute. The family who, according to her grandmother, were responsible for the death of Shayla's parents. How was that possible? *Why wasn't Draco on the list?* If it had been she'd have instantly made the connection and none of this would have happened.

She fought to keep from weeping. In a blink of the eye, something so spectacularly right had turned hideously wrong. It was as though the fates were conspiring against her. What next? Would her proposal to the Dantes also end in disaster because of her foolishness this night? Would Derek Algier call and tell her he'd changed his mind about hiring her? Would her precious chance at freedom evaporate with the coming of the morning sun?

Draco continued to wait for Shayla to answer his question,

looking hard and fierce and dangerously male, epitomizing the nature of his name. She moistened her lips, scrambling to come up with an excuse he'd buy.

"I guess there's nothing wrong with being a Dante," she conceded. Okay, lied. "I just… I didn't know and—"

He slowly relaxed, sliding back into his role of lover. "Got it. You're intimidated."

"Intimidated!" More than anything she wanted to escape the bed, but considering she'd be confronting the cocky bastard totally nude, she forced herself to stay put. She struggled to keep any hint of insult from her voice. "I'm not intimidated," she corrected with a calm she was far from feeling.

His hazel eyes narrowed, the gold flecks glittering a clear warning. "But for some reason, my being a Dante makes a difference."

She faltered, not quite certain how to respond, other than to use one small tidbit her grandmother had mentioned in passing. "The Dante men have something of a…reputation, shall we say?" Based on what just happened, a well-deserved reputation, she grudgingly admitted to herself. So, maybe he wasn't being cocky so much as honest.

"And you think that because I'm a Dante all I'm after is a one-night stand?"

It was a tad like the pot calling the kettle black, considering she'd been after just that, herself. Even so, she met his gaze unflinchingly. "Yes."

He shrugged. "Time will prove otherwise," he alarmed her by saying.

Dear heaven. He couldn't mean that, could he? But searching his expression she realized he meant precisely that. She crouched in a silken nest of rumpled sheets, at a total loss. What did she do now? How did she gracefully extricate herself from the situation? She wasn't interested in continuing a relationship with him after this one night, though caution dictated she not risk the loss of her fingers by feeding him that particular piece of information. She was also at a serious disadvantage since she was new to this type of situation. Maybe if she were more sexually experienced she could figure a way to soothe his male ego while she slipped out the door.

Before she had a chance to devise a plan, he caught her hand in his and tugged. Unmistakable want fired in his eyes. "Any other objections, sweetheart, or can we move on?"

More objections than she could possibly express. She needed to make a decision and fast, before he seduced her options right out of her. Either she left now, the smartest choice available to her, or she returned to his arms and allowed him to prove yet again what he did better—kiss or make love.

The first time with him she could rationalize. She hadn't known who he was. And then there had been that overpowering attraction. She stirred uneasily, aware that the warm throbbing in her palm hadn't diminished. Clearly, that attraction hadn't dissipated, despite discovering his full name. But she knew his identity now. His family had deliberately ruined hers, a fact that—according to Grandmother Charleston—had indirectly led to the death of her parents. Whatever the actual truth, the bankruptcy of her family's business had changed her life forever.

"Shayla?" Draco studied her expression. "Apparently you still have concerns. Maybe this will help."

Before she had time to protest, he leaned in, his passionate kiss the first taking. Then his hands took possession of her. He'd learned a lot about her during the few hours they'd been together, how to arouse her with a few clever strokes. And finally he took her under with his words, a tender suggestion that melted her resistance and made her hungry to experience his lovemaking again. Just one more time.

If she left now it wouldn't change anything. What was done was done. She couldn't regain what she'd given him even if she wanted to, any more than she could change how it would affect her meeting with his relatives. Tomorrow she'd turn twenty-five and wing her way out of the country. And truth be told, the memories of this night would linger in her thoughts for the rest of her life. Would it be so terrible to add to those memories, to stack up a few more to take with her when she left? To be mad and impetuous one last time? Who would know that she'd given herself to a Dante, other than herself? Well, and Draco.

Did she leave…or enjoy his lovemaking one more time? It was an easy decision to make.

Shayla surrendered with a sigh. The instant she reached for him and pulled him closer, heat ignited between them, dampening any lingering doubts. She'd spent a lifetime living according to her grandmother's dictates, focused first on her studies, then on making as much money as quickly as possible in order to repay her college expenses.

Come morning she'd complete her familial obligations by stepping into the role of family negotiator while she bartered with the Dantes. Once through, she'd bid Draco a fond farewell and claim her freedom. But tonight would be hers. An indulgence. The one-night stand she'd accused him of wanting and another step toward her independence.

Draco drew her under him and mated his body to hers in one swift move. She gasped as intense pleasure ripped her apart and scattered the pieces. She wrapped her legs around his waist and moved with him. Soared with him. Shot straight through the clouds and winged toward the searing heart of the sun, all within his arms. She heard the low rumble echo through his chest as his climax approached. Knowing she drove him so hard and high so quickly sent her tumbling up, teetering on a peak that had her gasping for breath, before launching into thin air in a delicious freefall.

"Draco…!" His name burst from her lungs in a half sob.

"I know, I know, I know," he chanted.

He drove home, losing himself in her heat. His head reared back and his throat convulsed. Then he said one single word. *Shayla*. He stamped it with such passion and possessiveness, it was as though he laid claim to her, changing the meaning so that it would forevermore be linked to him. Just as her body was linked to his. Just as her heart had become linked to his.

No. Oh, no, no, *no*.

She struggled to deny the possibility of it, scrambled for some other explanation. She was being foolish, caught up in the newness of their lovemaking, lost in a moment of intense desire. There was no connection, nothing to this Inferno that burned in her palm. Their joining was only temporary. Come morning she was leaving, and this night with Draco would fade to a fond and distant memory.

But even as she fought, sleep settled over her, just as she settled into the warmth of Draco's arms, accepting his possession. Accepting the rightness of his protective hold. She reached for him, cleaved to him. And with a tiny sigh of surrender, she linked her hand with his, palm to palm, cementing their bond.

When Shayla awoke she felt the morning through the darkness swathing the room and discovered Draco missing from the bed. She glanced toward the windows. They were tightly shuttered once again, delaying the advent of a new day—her birthday.

She stretched sore, abused muscles and sat up, shoving her hair from her face. Time to get up and leave. She had a lot to accomplish in the next few hours. But part of her regretted. Regretted the need to leave both the bed and the man. Regretted that she couldn't squeeze in one more day and night of pleasure. Before she could escape the bed, Draco returned to the room. It took only one look to realize something was terribly wrong. It also stripped her emotions bare. Acutely self-conscious, she covered herself with the sheet.

"Draco?" She despised the hint of nervousness that tripped through her voice and slithered down her spine. "Is there a problem?"

"Why don't we start with this?" Her beaded bag dangled from one hand. In the other he held the leather pouch.

Shayla stiffened in alarm. How could she have been so careless? Even more damning, how could she have let her purse and its precious contents out of her sight for even one short minute? She must have lost her mind. *Had* lost her mind the instant Draco had put his hands on her. His mouth on her. Had taken possession of her, body and soul.

He took a step toward her, moving from the shadows that enshrouded the outer edges of the room to a position beneath the recessed spotlights in his bedroom ceiling. The light haloed him, giving him the appearance of a dark angel bent on vengeance. Or maybe he'd transformed himself into the dragon for which he'd been named.

"That's my purse, as you well know." She held out her hand. "If you don't mind?"

"Oh, but I do mind." He untied the leather pouch, extracted one of the six parcel papers from inside and unfolded it. A diamond tumbled into his palm, burning with brilliance. "This is a fire diamond," he said.

Or was it an accusation? An odd roughness crisped the edges of his voice, something bitter-hot and laden with long-ago pain, the words overflowing with a subtext she couldn't begin to understand. But it was definitely there.

"How dare you rifle through my purse?" Her response escaped in heavily accented Southern affront. "You have no right—"

"These are all fire diamonds," he stated, more forcefully this time, the statement slicing like honed steel.

The overhead light gathered up the unmistakable sparkle captured within his palm and reflected the brilliance, seeming to fill the room with a fiery glitter—a glitter echoed in the equally fiery gold of Draco's eyes. What an idiot she'd been. This was no ordinary man. Those eyes. The hair. The stunning good looks and charm, a charm now eclipsed by a tough, ruthless edge. It all screamed Dante, even the ruthlessness, a quality her grandmother had long warned was endemic to his family. How terrifyingly ironic that she was now in a position to confirm that firsthand.

Shayla fought to speak past a throat gone bone-dry. "Yes," she finally said. "I do believe they are fire diamonds."

"What the *hell* are you doing with them?"

She escaped from the bed with as much dignity as she could muster, winding the sheet tightly around herself in order to preserve some shred of modesty. Ridiculous considering what they'd been busy doing all night and how many times and ways they'd done it. "They're mine. Give them back this minute."

His eyes narrowed. "Bull. Dantes doesn't sell loose fire diamonds. The only way to purchase them is set in jewelry. So, unless you were foolish enough to pry the diamonds out of their setting…?" He lifted an eyebrow in silent demand.

"I don't owe you an explanation. The diamonds belong to me and unless you can prove otherwise, I suggest you return them to where you found them."

She held out her hand and fixed him with an implacable

gaze. He didn't argue, which surprised her, but folded the diamond back into the blue-and-white parcel paper and returned it to the leather drawstring bag. Jerking the strings closed, he tucked it into her beaded purse and lobbed it toward her.

"You might want to get the clasp on that bag fixed. Everything fell out when I tossed your purse onto the couch last night."

"I'll get right on that." Relief flooded through her now that she had her handbag back in her possession, a very short-lived relief.

"And what about this?" He flipped up his index and middle fingers, a folded piece of paper tucked between them, a very damning piece of paper that listed the main Dante players and their job positions. "Care to explain this?"

How could she have forgotten the list? And of more urgent interest, why wasn't his name on it? Why hadn't he been mentioned in any of the Dante literature or internet research she and her grandmother had done? This morning just kept getting better and better. Gathering the shreds of her dignity, Shayla lifted her chin. "It's none of your business."

His expression iced over, assuming a merciless aspect. "When it comes to the Dantes, it's very much my business." He stepped closer. "You claimed you didn't know me. A lie, sweetheart?"

She refused to back down. "Did you see your name on that list?"

"Damn it, Shayla. What the *hell* is going on?"

"Nothing illicit," she retorted, stung. "It just happens that I have a meeting with certain members of your family today and I was dismayed when I discovered your identity because I didn't want a—" she almost said *one-night stand* and snatched back the words at the last possible second "—an intimate relationship with one Dante to affect my meeting with the others. That's why I crashed the reception last night. I wanted to get a look at who I'd be meeting today." Not that she'd managed even that. Instead, she'd allowed desire to get in the way of her promise to her grandmother. Shame filled her. "Just out of curiosity, why *wasn't* your name on my list?"

"I handle gemstones on a regular basis. Sometimes I carry them. For security reasons I prefer to remain off the grid. Now, about this meeting. Who, what and why, Shayla?" He snapped out the questions. "Not to mention, when?"

At the reminder, she inhaled sharply. "What time is it?"

"Nine."

"Oh, dear heaven." She scooped up her crumpled clothes from the floor and made a beeline for the bathroom. "I have to go. Now."

He caught her arm before she could escape the room. "Not until you explain what's going on."

Desire sizzled through her at his touch, a desire she fought to ignore with only limited success. "I'm not at liberty to explain. Nor do I owe you an explanation."

"Even after last night?"

She forced herself to meet his furious gaze, to cling to every ounce of self-control at her disposal. "Even after last night. One has nothing to do with the other."

"I disagree."

If only he weren't touching her. If only he'd let her go. "Please, Draco," she whispered. "I have to leave. Perhaps we could talk after the meeting."

He continued to hold her and she could tell he waged an inner debate, though she didn't have a clue what he was thinking. Last night he'd been so open and giving, so generous in the way he'd made love to her. In the space of a few minutes he'd gone from the man with whom she'd shared unbearable emotional intimacy to someone hard and ferocious. She shivered. A dragon in fact, as well as name.

"Get dressed." He released her arm, but for some reason the desire didn't ebb as she expected. "Then I'll see you out."

She flinched. Without another word she crossed to the bathroom and shut the door with a decisive click. After a quick shower, she pulled on her gown from the previous night, struggling against a wave of humiliation at wearing an evening dress during daylight hours. She'd return to her dingy little motel room in the previous night's finery, looking like…

Color swept into her face and she deliberately clamped down on every stray thought and emotion. She used Draco's comb to yank the tangles from her hair. Without her clips she couldn't put it up and she most certainly wasn't going out there and scramble around on the floor looking for them. Shoving her feet into her heels, she exited the bathroom.

Draco stood at the threshold leading to the hallway, leaning a shoulder against the doorjamb. He'd used the time she'd been in the bathroom to dress, though in far more casual clothes than what she had available. He'd also chosen unrelieved black; the only color the hard gold glitter of his eyes.

"Would you mind calling me a cab?" she asked with a calm she was far from feeling.

"Already done." He swept a hand in the general direction of the living room and—hallelujah—the exit. "After you."

She hesitated a split second, then led with her chin. Crossing the room, she paused in the doorway, waiting for him to move out of her path. He didn't. He simply watched and waited, no doubt curious to see what she'd do. Well, her grandmother hadn't raised a coward. Shayla might have made some improper choices the night before, but by God she'd own them and take the consequences.

Without a word, she pressed past him. Just that brief contact stirred a storm of emotion. Memories of their night together spun through her, making her dizzy with the sensations they roused. The way Draco had caressed her. The lingering kisses he'd feathered across every inch of her body. The strength of his hold. The way he'd taken her, easing her passage, managing to be powerful and tender and giving all at the same time.

She'd never forget how it had been with him, nor the fact that he was the first man to make love to her. He'd changed her, indelibly branding her. He was part of her and always would be. The thought filled her with anxiety and she tucked it away for some future time when she could take it out and analyze it with the attention it deserved.

Draco shifted and the moment passed, even if the remnants still clung. He called for the elevator and keyed it in for the garage level. At her startled glance, he lifted a shoulder. "Even though it's Saturday, I didn't think you'd appreciate making the Walk of Shame through the main reception area for Dantes' corporate offices, especially if you have a meeting with Sev and Primo later today. You never know who you may run into."

Oh, God, please don't let her cry at his thoughtfulness. "Thank you," she whispered. "I appreciate your consideration."

"I arranged for the cab to meet us at the side entrance. With luck no one will know you spent the night with me. Although…"

She glanced up at him in alarm. "Although?"

"My grandfather, Primo, has a knack for hearing what you'd like to keep quiet."

"My grandmother is the same way." Though she couldn't

imagine how Leticia Charleston might possibly discover that Shayla had slept with the enemy. "I'd prefer it if this could be our secret."

The doors slid open and Draco stepped in front of her, preventing her escape. "Just out of curiosity, would you have slept with me if I'd told you from the start that I was a Dante?"

She didn't bother to sugarcoat it. "No."

Draco's expression hardened and he gave a curt nod. "Thought so. Unfortunately, you've neglected to take into consideration one small detail."

Escape. She just wanted to escape. She stared longingly over his shoulder toward the exit. "What's that?"

He startled her by taking her hand in his, allowing the heat to pulse between them. "The Inferno has other plans for you."

Releasing her, they exited the elevator. He escorted her across the concrete garage toward a steel door that opened onto a side street. Her stiletto heels echoed with every step while the throb centered in her palm matched the rhythmic tempo. A cab stood waiting. Ever the gentleman, Draco held the door for her and helped her in.

"Where to?" he asked.

Until that moment, it hadn't occurred to her that she might have to tell him the name of her motel. But it made perfect sense. He'd want to know where to track her down. One glance at his set expression warned that he hadn't finished saying all he intended to about their night together. Since she couldn't bring herself to mention the fleabag where she'd booked her room, she chose the only other viable option. She lied.

"I'm staying at the Mark Hopkins," she said.

Leaning into the front passenger window, Draco handed the driver a couple of folded bills. "The Mark," he repeated.

And then he stepped back, his gaze fixed on her. This time she didn't have a bit of trouble reading his expression. Both threat and promise were implicit in his hazel eyes.

Three

The minute the cab pulled away and vanished around a corner, Draco reached into his pocket and palmed the diamond concealed there.

The stone pressed into his skin, hard and cold, and yet brimming with fire. He pulled it out and studied the flash of color. No question that it was a fire diamond, though something about it looked different. Off. Until he could analyze it in the lab he wouldn't be able to say what. Nor would he be able to tell if it was one of the six he'd been swindled out of all those years ago. Stones he'd spent a solid decade tracking down, diamond by damnable diamond, until only two were still missing.

One thing he knew beyond a shadow of a doubt. If this diamond had anything to do with Shayla's appointment at Dantes, he intended to be there. In fact, if Primo and Sev had known about the diamonds, they'd have insisted he attend. In the meantime, he'd analyze the stone before he crashed the party, and see if the information he gained wouldn't give them some small advantage in whatever negotiations were imminent.

He stopped by the receptionist's desk on the way to the lab. The company always arranged for someone to man the station over the weekend since many Dantes events occurred then. Or they often had guests in one or more of the penthouse suites who might require assistance during their stay.

"'Morning, Laura."

She greeted him with a friendly smile. "Hello, Mr. Dante. What can I do for you?"

"What time are Primo and Sev arriving for the meeting with Shayla?" He paused. "Damn. Forgot her last name."

"Hang on. I have it here." She called up a calendar on her computer with a punch of a button. "Charleston. Shayla Charleston. The meeting is scheduled to begin at ten-thirty. They'll be using the Jade conference room."

Perfect. An hour would give him just enough time to prepare. "Give me a call when Ms. Charleston arrives, will you? I'll be in the lab."

"Certainly, Mr. Dante."

As it turned out, it didn't take long for the preliminary assessment. What he discovered stunned him. He was fairly certain it would also stun his grandfather, Primo, and his cousin, Sev. Shortly after Laura alerted him to everyone's arrival, Draco entered the conference room through a side door.

Shayla sat in profile. She had presence, he'd give her that, capturing everyone's attention without even trying. She'd once again swept her mass of dark hair into an elegant knot and wore a crisp, tailored skirt and jacket, the lemony color adding a ray of sunshine in contrast to the more somber suits and ties. He couldn't place the designer, but it was definitely a high-priced label, just as her evening gown had been.

He caught Sev's eye and gave him a signal indicating he wanted to sit in on the meeting. His cousin nodded and Draco took a chair at the opposite end of the table from Shayla, beside his grandfather. He suppressed a smile when she studiously avoided looking his way, a fact noted by several of his relatives.

If she wanted to keep their relationship a secret, she was going about it the exact wrong way. She should have acknowledged him. By ignoring him, she might as well have put up a huge sign saying, "We slept together, but I don't want anyone to figure it out." And his sign would say, "Too late. They just have and Primo is *not* happy."

As though to bring home his point, Primo placed a hand on Draco's shoulder, and growled in Italian, "Why must you always be the troublemaker? Explain this to me."

Draco didn't bother trying to explain it. How could he explain something that came as naturally as breathing? Answering in Italian, he simply stated, "She's mine."

Primo's shaggy gray brows shot upward and his hard gold eyes widened. "So Rafe was not the only one Inferno-struck last night."

Draco kept his expression bland. Apparently his brother had taken his suggestion and faked a run-in with The Inferno with Larkin Thatcher. That would prove interesting. "I guess not." He shoved back his chair and stood. "If you'll excuse me, Primo?"

Since it was readily apparent to everyone at the table that he and Shayla were involved, there was no point in pretending. He circled the table and took the chair next to her.

"What are you doing?" she murmured beneath her breath. Alarm rippled through the question. "Get away from me."

"They already know."

"I'm well aware of that fact. Primo made it abundantly clear. But you don't have to rub it in their faces."

She'd caught him by surprise. "You speak Italian?"

"And several other languages, as well." She continued to avoid meeting his gaze. "What I don't understand is why you felt the need to tell them about last night."

"I didn't. You did."

A blush mounted her cheeks. "I most certainly did not." Her Southern accent deepened, blurring her words. "I never said a blessed thing."

"You didn't have to say anything. Let's just say you have an expressive face."

She started to say something, then broke off and snatched a quick breath. "Okay, fine. I'll just have to deal with the embarrassment and stay focused on business."

Embarrassment? For some reason the word irritated the hell out of him. He struggled to keep his voice pitched low. "Why does it embarrass you that we were together last night?" He gathered her hand in his, feeling the flare of The Inferno when their fingers collided and meshed and their palms bumped together. "For that matter, why does it matter what my family suspects? Unless one of us confirms it, they won't know for certain."

"You're touching me. Mix that with whispering and you get a bucket load of guilt."

"Odd. I don't feel the least guilty. Or embarrassed."

He leaned on the final word, hoping for a reaction. And got one. She made the mistake of looking directly at him and he felt that look arrow straight to his groin. It was a wonder the air didn't combust between them. She must have read his reaction in his expression.

"Darn it, Draco. Cut that out. Go sit somewhere else."

"Can't." It was the God's honest truth. No way in hell was he going to stand and provide proof of his attraction for her.

Comprehension had her color deepening. "Why are you

at this meeting?" she asked in despair. "Why couldn't you have had the decency to stay away?"

"Maybe I would have if it hadn't been for this…"

He opened his hand, revealing the diamond he'd taken from her. He'd put it in a protective Lucite box and sent the box shooting toward the center of the conference table. It spun dead center, the diamond inside spitting out shards of brilliant color, igniting the fire buried in its depth.

"It would seem Ms. Charleston has something interesting to show us," Draco informed his family.

Sev snatched up the case and studied it. "Son of a— It's a fire diamond." His gaze narrowed on Shayla, filled with suspicion. "Where did you get this?"

"It's not one of ours," Draco offered helpfully.

Dead silence greeted his comment. "What do you mean it is not ours?" Primo finally demanded. "How is this possible?"

"It is, indeed, a fire diamond," Draco confirmed. "But it doesn't come from one of our mines. Which begs the question…" He swiveled his chair so it faced Shayla. "Where the hell did it come from?"

She'd put the few minutes he'd given her to good use, wrapping herself in an artificial calm. "That diamond, as well as the others in my possession, came from a Charleston mine."

Lazz, the family's CFO, frowned. "I thought your mines were played out years ago."

And that's when it clicked. Draco stiffened. Charleston. Shayla Charleston. As in…Charlestons, the now-defunct jewelry empire. They'd been in direct competition with Dantes decades ago until poor management and the inability to compete against Dantes' fire diamonds had driven them out of business.

"We also thought the mines were played out. A recent

survey has proven that not only aren't they depleted, but they contain fire diamonds." She leaned forward to emphasize her point. "Fire diamonds superior to the Dantes'."

"That's not possible," Sev objected.

She set the leather bag on the table in front of her. "This is a small sample of what we've extracted. Let me repeat that—a *small* sample. You're welcome to examine them at your leisure. I realize it'll take time."

Primo waved his hand toward Draco, indicating he should take care of the analysis and grading. "So." He leaned back in his chair and folded his arms across his chest. "Letty has her own supply of fire diamonds. I am surprised she is giving us advance warning of her intentions. Or is it more in the nature of a threat?"

He tilted his head to one side, and fixed the power of his gaze on Shayla. Draco had seen men of immense power and position crumble beneath that gaze. But not Shayla. She met him look for look.

"It's not a warning, Mr. Dante, or a threat." Her smile flickered to life. Draco considered it one of her most potent weapons. "It's a proposition. My grandmother is offering you the exclusive opportunity to lease our mines."

Sev focused his gaze on Shayla as well, one identical to his grandfather's. "Why?"

"It's quite simple. We're not in the business anymore. My parents, who probably could have revitalized Charlestons, are dead and I have neither the interest nor the ability to run the company," she admitted with endearing candor. "To be blunt, we simply aren't in the position to mine the stones or cut them—other than this initial lot—let alone create jewelry with them. You are."

Primo weighed the information for a long moment before speaking. "There are others who would pay your grandmother a fortune for the mining rights. Competitors of Dantes. Considering she has always blamed us for putting Charlestons out of business and it is in her nature to exact revenge…" He spread his hands wide and shrugged. "Why does she not use this opportunity to her advantage?"

"My grandmother is older now. Losing my parents hit her hard."

Primo nodded. "I heard about the accident. Having lost one of my own sons, along with his wife, I can sympathize with Letty. But it is your loss that grieves me most."

Tears welled in her eyes and she blinked them back, impressing the hell out of Draco with her control. "Thank you."

Primo inclined his head. "Would you be offended if we discuss the situation in Italian?"

"Not at all." She sent him a charming smile. "Would you be offended if I listened in?"

Primo stilled. "You speak Italian?"

"*Parlo italiano fluente*," she admitted.

"Fluently and with an excellent accent," Draco murmured. Then he raised his voice. "In that case… Shayla, would you mind waiting in my office while my family and I discuss the situation?"

She slid back her chair and stood. "Not at all."

Draco escorted her from the conference room and down the hallway to his office. "Help yourself to coffee," he offered. "I made a fresh pot a short time ago."

Before she could guess his intentions he leaned in for a swift kiss. Their lips joined, parted, then met again for a slower, more thorough exploration. Her breath sighed from her lungs, filled with hunger, yet shaded with regret. He wished there were time for more than a swift, stolen kiss. But his family waited and he didn't doubt for a minute that if he delayed any longer they'd guess why.

"I have to go," he reluctantly informed her.

She drew back. "And we shouldn't be mixing business with pleasure, anyway."

"We'll have plenty of time for pleasure later," he reassured her. "Once this is settled."

She turned abruptly. "I look forward to hearing your family's decision," she said.

Her formality amused him, given what they'd been doing a few short hours earlier. "It shouldn't take long."

He returned to the conference room, interrupting a heated exchange between his cousins, who debated Leticia Charleston's motivations for her offer. No one commented on the delay, though Primo pulled out a cigar and swept him with a quick, encompassing stare as he lit up, breaking more California laws and codes than Draco cared to consider.

While the debate continued to rage, Draco leaned back in his chair and took it all in. He wished he remembered more of the history between the Dantes and the Charlestons and made a point of researching the facts as soon as possible. But one small detail captured his full attention.

Primo described Leticia Charleston as a vengeful woman.

Draco understood that quality. Possessed that quality. Intended to exercise his thirst for vengeance to the fullest when he found the person responsible for swindling him out of a half dozen of Dantes' finest and rarest fire diamonds, an event that had taken place a full decade before. He'd been all of twenty at the time and overinflated with his own self-importance, eager to prove himself. That single mistake had changed him.

Permanently.

Primo often referred to him as the Dante troublemaker, but that wasn't quite accurate. Draco was possibly the most deceptive of the Dantes since he hid certain elements of his personality behind a congenial, mischievous mask. But he found he could easily slip into Leticia's shoes and consider the matter from her point of view. Analyze how best she might go about destroying the Dantes.

Conversation wafted over him while his family discussed their options. Once Draco satisfied himself that he'd weighed all the possibilities, he lifted a finger. Silence descended.

Primo waved his cigar in Draco's direction. Smoke sketched the path his hand had taken. "Speak."

"Let's start with what we know," he suggested. "First off, Leticia Charleston wants to alert us to the fact that she now owns a supply of fire diamonds. Based on an admittedly quick examination, I'm forced to concur with what Shayla told us. At first blush, they appear superior to ours."

"But they're real? They haven't been treated?"

"Yes, they're real," Draco said in response to Sev's questions. "And no, they haven't been treated. Unfortunately, I can't give you more specifics until I've had time to run them through a full analysis other than to say that, with a few rare exceptions, they're better than what we have."

Ferocious denial exploded around him. Sev's voice cut across them all. "You can't be serious."

"I'm dead serious," Draco replied. Since he was the expert, there wasn't much they could say to refute the claim, though they wanted to. Badly. "Second. She's offering us first refusal to lease her mines. Why?" He fixed his gaze on his grandfather. "There's bad blood between us. And you described her as a vengeful woman."

Primo took his time blowing out a stream of aromatic smoke. "Cold. Bitter. A nasty creature."

Coming from Primo it was a damning condemnation. Draco nodded. "As mentioned, she could easily peddle her diamonds to any of our competitors. But the best I can figure, she came to us for one reason."

"Which is?" Lazz asked impatiently.

"This gives her a sword to hold over our heads. If we don't dance to her tune, she drops the sword and sells her stones elsewhere. The power and control are hers to wield. For as long as her mines cough up diamonds that trump our own, she can name her price and we'll pay it. Otherwise Dantes loses its status as the only jewelry empire in the world to possess fire diamonds. Worse, if she eventually chooses to sell to our competitors, to all our competitors *except* us," he emphasized, "we'll have a lower grade of diamonds than everyone else possesses. Our fall from grace will be abrupt and hard—"

"—and no doubt be met with tears of joy from jewelers around the world," Sev said sourly.

Lazz nodded in agreement. "Ultimately, it could put us in a very precarious position, business-wise."

"It is logical," Primo agreed.

"If we don't nail the Charleston woman to an ironclad contract, she'll screw us over," Sev stated. "She'll play her game until it bores her and then sell elsewhere."

Primo sighed wearily. "I am forced to admit, it would be in keeping with her nature."

"Then we agree to lease her mines?"

Lazz shook his head. "We agree to examine the stones and insist on our own survey of the mines. We investigate the offer top-to-bottom and then push for the best possible terms."

Sev grimaced. "I suspect the best possible is going to be damn poor."

Draco didn't disagree. "So, we take it one step at a time and see if we can't figure out a way to beat the Charleston woman at her own game."

"And what about Shayla?" Primo's question dropped like a boulder onto a mirror-calm lake, sending out huge, disruptive waves. He studied the tip of his glowing cigar. "I am forced to wonder...what is her purpose in all this? Letty has always blamed us for the death of her son. Does the granddaughter also blame us? Does Shayla have the same thirst for vengeance as her grandmother?"

Draco turned on his grandfather. "Are we responsible for her father's death?"

Primo shook his head. "No more than we are responsible for the depletion of the Charleston mines. But there is much you do not know, much I can explain at a more appropriate time." He flicked ash from his cigar toward an ashtray. "But that does not mean that Shayla does not blame, that she has not been taught to blame. We must give serious consideration to her role in this chess match."

"Shayla's role is quite simple. She's mine." The words escaped before Draco could control them. But he meant every one of them. "She has nothing to do with this."

"She has everything to do with this," Lazz insisted. "She's the one who approached us, not Leticia. How do you know she didn't seduce you as part of her grandmother's plan?"

Primo grimaced. "This troubles me, as well. Though my instinct says Shayla is a good person, we do not yet know her nature well enough to judge whether she hides a thirst for revenge behind the congenial mask she wears."

Draco literally saw red, the heat of it blurring the edges of his vision. It took every ounce of self-control to keep from vaulting across the table and decking someone. "She isn't hiding behind a mask," he rasped out in reply. "She's not like that."

"You've only known her one night!" Lazz snapped.

Draco held out his hand, palm up. "We were chosen for each other."

Sev interrupted, stemming Lazz's simmering retort. "We have to consider every possibility, Draco. Surely you must see that? From what Primo has said, I wouldn't put anything past

Leticia Charleston. Until we see how this plays out, Shayla is suspect. At the very least it puts the two of you on opposite sides of an intensely adversarial business deal."

"Then we'll keep business separate from our personal relationship," Draco shot back.

"I've been there with Francesca and, trust me, it wasn't pretty," his cousin replied, referring to his own experiences when he and his wife first met. "My situation was bad enough. What you're dealing with will be far worse."

Draco shrugged. "So I'll deal."

"And if we have to take the Charlestons down?" Lazz asked. "How will Shayla react to that? For that matter, how will you?"

Draco didn't hesitate. "You know my first loyalty is to my family. When Shayla becomes my wife, her loyalty will be to me, which means to the Dantes."

Lazz snorted, and he and Sev exchanged ironic glances. "You don't know women very well, do you?"

"I know Shayla that well."

"After just one night?" Sev asked skeptically.

Draco climbed to his feet and confronted his cousins. "How long did it take you and Francesca, Sev? I seem to remember it was all of one night." His gaze switched to Lazz. "What about you and Ariana? You may have resisted longer and harder, but in the end you still fell."

Lazz blew out a sigh. "You're that certain?"

Draco didn't hesitate. "Yes."

Sev nodded, though he didn't look happy. "I guess the real question is…does Shayla feel the same way?"

Once again, Draco didn't hesitate. "If she doesn't now, she will in time, once she's had a chance to come to terms with what's happened." He lifted an eyebrow. "Unless you're saying The Inferno doesn't work."

Sev released a humorless laugh. "Oh, it works. You'll

discover just how well soon enough. My concern is whether she's about to become a pawn in this battle, trapped between her loyalty to her grandmother and her feelings for you."

Draco had already considered that possibility. "If she is, she'll be the first piece I capture," he stated firmly. "Whatever it takes to remove her from the playing field. But I *will* protect what's mine."

The meeting didn't last much longer. They invited Shayla back into the conference room and assured her of their interest in pursuing her grandmother's proposition. They requested another survey of the mines, which she readily agreed to. They asked for time to examine the diamonds. Since she'd already suggested as much, she didn't argue that, either. Finally, they asked for a copy of the proposed lease along with any conditions pertaining to it and Shayla promised that her grandmother's lawyer would fax it to them within the week.

To Draco's amusement he watched Shayla charm the men, his grandfather and cousins falling, one by one, beneath the enchantment of her smile and her sunny personality. It wasn't a deliberate maneuver on her part. He'd have caught it if she'd been playing them. He suspected Primo would have, as well. In fact, his grandfather watched Shayla with an eagle eye, careful to reassure himself that this particular apple had fallen well away from the poisoned tree of her grandmother.

The instant the meeting wrapped, Draco whisked Shayla off to his office. "Why don't you come upstairs and have lunch with me," he suggested the moment they were safely closeted inside.

"Not a chance," she said with a small grin. "I have a feeling 'come upstairs and have lunch' is your code for 'come upstairs and take your clothes off.'"

"Well… We could do that, too. I wouldn't mind eating

lunch naked, so long as it's with you." He approached, snagging the lapels of her lemony suit jacket and reeling her in. "Of course, we can also get naked right here in my office. You'll find my couch is extremely comfortable."

She shook her head, unable to suppress a laugh. "As tempting as your offer is, I'll pass." Her amusement faded, replaced by a bittersweet longing. "I'm really sorry, Draco, but I have to go."

"Time to report in to your grandmother?" He tried to keep the edge from his voice with only limited success.

She must have picked up on it, because she met his look dead-on, a hint of defiance glittering in the darkness. "Among other things, yes."

He let it go, determined to tip them over that line from business straight into pleasure, and keep them there. "Why don't we have dinner together?" he suggested. "Somewhere ridiculously expensive and romantic. We'll celebrate a new alliance between the Charlestons and the Dantes."

She avoided his gaze. "A little premature to celebrate an alliance, don't you think?" she asked. "There's a lot of work to accomplish before a lease is signed."

He meant them and their relationship, not the lease, though there didn't seem any point in explaining that fact. Instead, he schooled himself to patience. She didn't understand about The Inferno and what was happening between them. Not yet. Until she did, until she accepted, he needed to take it slow.

"We can fight the past, or accept it and move on." Coming from him, that particular philosophy was almost funny, since he'd spent ten endless years fighting to right a single long-ago wrong. "What happens in the future is up to you. To us."

She released her breath in a drawn-out sigh. "You're right." She turned with a smile, though it didn't contain her usual cheerfulness. He could still see regret lurking around the edges. "Where and when do you want to meet?"

"I'll pick you up at the Mark."

She shook her head. "I'd rather meet you at the restaurant." Her expression turned provocative. "But if you promise not to behave yourself, I'll let you take me home."

His eyebrows winged upward. "*Not* to behave myself?"

She simply looked at him and waited.

Hell, he could do that. He was an expert at not behaving. "Done," he agreed. He didn't get it then. He should have. But he was so desperate to have her again, the little cues went right over his head. "There's a terrific seafood place in North Beach. Do you know where North Beach is?"

"Between Fisherman's Wharf and Chinatown," she answered promptly.

"I'm impressed."

She shrugged it off. "Don't be. I did some exploring before the reception. It's a wonder I could squeeze my poor abused feet into those heels considering how much walking I did."

"Well, I'm glad you managed, since I had such fun taking them off. In fact, I had fun taking off all of your bits and pieces." He couldn't resist touching her again. Kissing her. Gathering her into his arms, where she belonged. She didn't resist, but snuggled in, returning his kiss as though they'd been parted for months, instead of hours. "Meet me at Cocina at eight," he said, when they finally came up for air.

"Draco…"

Somehow her hair had come loose again and he filled his hands with it, allowing it to trickle through his fingers. "Stay," he murmured against her mouth.

"I wish…" She broke off and pulled free of his embrace. Putting some distance between them, she shook her head. "I can't."

He caught an odd emotion rippling across her expression. "Shayla?" Something wasn't right, but he couldn't quite put his finger on it. "What is it, sweetheart?"

She gathered herself with a visible effort. "I'm sorry. I really have to go."

If only he'd pushed a little harder. If only he'd been paying closer attention. But he hadn't. Didn't. And so the moment passed. "I understand." He checked his watch. "Hell, it's hours before I'll see you again. Are you sure you don't want to meet up sooner?"

"Yes." She closed her eyes with a soft exclamation. "I'd love to, but I can't. Draco, you have to let me go. I'll see you at eight."

She darted forward and wrapped her arms around his neck and kissed him, kissed him with a desperate passion. Clung like she'd never let him go. Sighed like a woman in love. He went under with her, losing himself in an embrace that promised everything, but still left him empty-handed when she slipped away and, without another word, exited the room.

The day stretched long and lonely, inching toward the appointed time they'd agreed to meet. He arrived a full fifteen minutes early. Shayla was running late. More than eight months late, as it turned out. But Draco didn't know that then.

After a full hour of pulverizing breadsticks, he was forced to face facts. She wasn't coming. He threw down a wad of cash and headed for the Mark, where the snooty reservationist on duty informed him that there was no Shayla Charleston staying with them. Had never been a Shayla Charleston staying with them. And could he please step aside so that *paying* customers might be assisted.

Next, Draco placed a call to Leticia Charleston, who claimed she had no knowledge of her granddaughter's whereabouts and no, she couldn't be bothered to pass on a message. She ended the conversation by informing him that any further contact should be through her attorney...unless, of course, the Dantes were no longer interested in leasing her mines.

Draco's final call was to Juice, a former associate of his brother, Luc. Juice specialized in background checks, finding what others didn't want found, and all things stored in cyberspace. "I have a job for you," Draco informed him the instant the call went through.

"What is it with you Dantes?" Juice's deep bass voice rumbled in his ear. "You don't know how to say, 'Hello'? Even a quick, 'How ya doin'?' But, no. It's always, 'I need some info and I need it yesterday.' First your brother, Rafe, hits me up last night, now you tonight."

Draco fought for patience. "Hello. How ya doin'? I need some info and I need it yesterday. I want you to dig up everything you can on a Shayla Charleston. Then I want you to find her for me."

"I'm not sure I like the way you say 'find her,' my man."

It had been an endless night and Draco's control finally snapped. "What's the way I said it have to do with anything?" he snarled.

"That depends. First, you best remember you're the one asking for a favor." He let that sink in.

Draco swore. "I'm sorry, Juice. She's…" She's what? His Inferno mate? Apparently not since she'd walked away from what they'd had. "She's important."

"Inferno, important?"

Draco didn't bother to deny it. "Yeah."

"Well, okay then. That brings us to my second question. What happens to the girl once I track her down?"

Hell. "Either I put a wedding ring on her finger or she's going to wish we'd never met."

"Huh. Sounds to me like you're tempted to do both."

"That's a distinct possibility," Draco growled.

"I'll have her for you within the week," Juice promised.

"But if you don't mind me saying, I suggest you seriously consider pursuing option one, rather than option two."

Draco glared down at the phone. "And why is that?"

"Because you and I would have to have a serious conversation if you decide on option two. And trust me, you don't want that to happen."

With that, the phone went dead. Draco closed his eyes and swore again, more virulently this time. He'd never hurt Shayla, not when he was honor-bound to protect her. She was his mate. He was worried. Concerned. He needed to find her, discover why she'd stood him up. Was it because of her grandmother? Because he was a Dante? Or something else… something worse? Until he found her, he'd never know.

But all the while, Lazz's question ran through his mind like a broken recording. *How do you know she didn't seduce you as part of her grandmother's plan?* Draco shook his head. No. It couldn't have been a setup. She didn't know who he was when they'd met. The others, sure. But not him. His name hadn't been on the list. She'd been patently shocked when he told her he was a Dante.

But… What if he was wrong? What if history was repeating itself and he'd once again fallen for a clever con?

Damn it to hell!

Draco's palm throbbed and he rubbed it with his thumb. He'd thought The Inferno had forged a permanent connection between them. Now he wondered. Maybe it had worked, but only on him. Maybe his Inferno connector was on the fritz. Maybe he'd be the first to find his soul mate, only to discover that she didn't feel the same way.

Perfect. Draco Dante, the only member of his entire family to screw up The Inferno. *Porca vacca!* He really was trouble.

Four

Nine months later...

Draco had lost Shayla in the fading glory of summer and found her again in the burgeoning promise of a fertile spring. But he did find her, though it had taken Juice far longer than the week he'd anticipated. How ironic that it was here, hiding out in her family home, where he'd started his search.

The Charleston house stood at the end of a long drive, an ancient antebellum mansion best seen from a kind distance. The closer Draco came, the more apparent the ravages of time, despite the flowering trees and perennials that attempted to disguise the slow decline into rot. The mansion stood exposed, shimmering through the humidity beneath a merciless and unforgiving sun. He didn't understand it. The handful of diamonds Shayla had shown him could have more than transformed the place. So, why hadn't they put the money the Dantes had paid for them to good use?

An ancient housekeeper opened the door and shuffled him along to a shabby parlor, where he was formally announced. Leticia Charleston responded by leveling a glare at the housekeeper, no doubt because she'd had the effrontery to permit a Dante across her precious threshold. Caving to the inevitable, Leticia waved Draco toward a high-backed chair decorated in faded damask. He ignored the invitation to sit.

"As I've informed you each time you've phoned, Mr. Dante, Shayla is not here."

As badly as he wanted to call her a liar, his family continued to do business with the woman, though now they were locked in fierce negotiations to purchase the mines, rather than to lease them. Ticking her off was not in Dantes' best interest. Unfortunately, he wasn't the most charming of Primo's grandchildren. That honor went to his cousin, Marco.

Worse, after so many months of searching, Draco's temper was worn down to a small, jagged nub. The least wrong word caused him to shoot first, talk later. Unfortunately once the hapless transgressor went down in flames it didn't leave a lot of room for discussion. And as appealing as the image of Shayla's grandmother being turned to a pile of ash was, he needed to try for a more diplomatic approach.

"She's here," he nearly growled.

So much for diplomacy.

Leticia lifted a perfectly drawn eyebrow a shade darker than her perfectly styled, deep gold hair. Now he could tell where her funds had been channeled. For a woman in her early seventies, she looked spectacular on the outside, even if the inner corrosion ran strong and deep. It would seem the decayed exterior of the house reflected the personality of its mistress.

"Are you calling me a liar?" she demanded.

He glared at her, dragon to dragon. "I believe if you'll

take a look in one of those half-dozen bedrooms upstairs, you'll find your missing granddaughter." He shot a grim look around the cavernous room. "Considering the size of this place I can understand you accidentally misplacing her. But if you need me to help look…?" He lifted his own eyebrow, one as black as soot.

"A *half*-dozen? I'll have you know there are a *full* dozen bedrooms upstairs, none of which contain my granddaughter. Shayla is not some princess I'm keeping locked away in a tower, despite what you clearly believe. And you are most certainly not a prince, but some ill-mannered creature possessing not an ounce of civilized behavior." Leticia shot to her feet and gestured toward the door leading to the hallway… and the way out. "Now, if you don't mind?"

"Here's the problem." He planted his feet firmly atop a handmade Tabriz carpet that still carried a whiff of lost elegance. Then he folded his arms across his chest. "I do mind. I mind very much."

Leticia stuck out a chin identical to her granddaughter's, fire burning in eyes as blue as Shayla's were black. Her only show of nerves was the way she gripped a ring dangling from a gold chain strung around her neck. Based on the glitter of diamonds, he suspected it was her wedding ring, though why she wore it around her neck instead of on her finger he couldn't begin to guess. Maybe widows in the South did it that way.

"She's not here," Leticia informed him. As though aware she'd exposed her anxiety, she tucked her ring away beneath her elegant silk blouse.

Draco met her, chin for jaw, putting a spark of fire in his own hazel-gold eyes. "Yes, she is."

He didn't know who would have caved first if a voice hadn't interrupted the standoff. "Grandmother? I need your opinion." The sound of her came like a sip of water to a parched and desperate desert. Painfully slow footsteps crossed the cypress floorboards of the foyer, heading straight for the parlor and sounding like the ring of destiny. "Oh, I'm sorry. I didn't realize you had company."

Leticia fell back into her chair with a word that had Draco's brows shooting skyward, while her expression soured, threatening to destroy all the hard work of her plastic surgeon. "Why, it's a miracle. My beloved granddaughter has appeared out of thin air after all these long months." She bit off each word as if it was acid in her mouth and drummed her synthetic nails against the armrest of her chair. "Hallelujah and kill the fatted calf."

Draco spared her a sardonic look before turning. "Hello, Shayla."

He heard the sharp catch of her breath the instant she realized who he was. "Draco."

His name escaped on a current of emotions, only a few of which he could identify. Disbelief. Wonder. An underscoring of pain. He could understand the disbelief since she'd run so long and hard to escape him. But the other two left him bewildered.

She stood a few steps inside the parlor, as though poised to vanish as unexpectedly as she'd appeared. She held two small, crocheted blankets clutched to her chest, one a bright and cheerful yellow, the other a tumble of rainbow colors. She looked different than he remembered, softer. More country casual than city chic. Sweet and oh, so not-so innocent.

Maybe it was her hair, which she wore pulled back from her face and fastened with two clips so it sheeted down her back in an inky waterfall. Or maybe it was her dress, at least what he could see of it around the blankets she held. It was simple ivory, pleated at the neckline and flowing, long and loose, to her calves.

None of the differences mattered, he knew that much for

certain. All that mattered was the hard joyous thrum of The Inferno and the relentless kick of desire, the intensity building to a fever pitch now that he was finally face-to-face with her. He'd have snatched her in his arms, except for one small detail.

In the past months he'd come to the conclusion that Lazz was right. His Inferno mate had screwed him over—literally and figuratively—no doubt at the behest of her grandmother.

"Hello, Shayla." There were so many things he wanted to say to her. So many things he planned to get off his chest once he found her. But standing there, staring at her, he couldn't think of one damn word of his entire speech. "It's been a while."

"I guess you're here to talk to my grandmother about the purchase contracts." She took a swift step backward. "I'll leave you to it."

"I'm not here to see your grandmother." He approached, not the least surprised by the alarm building in her dark gaze. It had been a long, difficult chase, but she'd just been trapped and he didn't intend to release her anytime soon. "I'm here to talk to you."

"This really isn't a good time," she began, taking another swift step backward.

She clutched the blankets in a white-knuckle grip, holding them almost protectively against her chest. It was her profound nervousness, bordering on fear, that finally gave her away. He looked at her this time. Really looked. And then it was his turn for his breath to hitch. His turn to stare in stunned disbelief.

"You're pregnant." The words escaped, part statement, part accusation.

From behind him, he heard Leticia moan. "Shayla,

you're *pregnant*? Why didn't you tell your poor, dear grand-mamma?"

Shayla's confused gaze darted from him to her grandmother and back again. "Yes, I'm pregnant. I guess that means there's cause for celebration all around. I understand you're married, Draco. Congratulations."

Married? "Who the hell told you that?" he snarled, though he could guess.

"My grandmother."

He suspected that if she'd thought first she might not have given him an honest answer. "Did she?"

Naturally, the old woman continued to brazen it out. "That's what I heard." She rolled her eyes. "But what do I know? You Dantes breed like rabbits. With so many to choose from, it's possible I got the name of the groom wrong."

"That tears it." He shot her a blistering glare that had her shrinking back against the cushions of her chair. "I don't care if this is your house, I want you out of this room right now."

"Well, I never!" Leticia said, playing the affronted grand dame to the hilt.

"Then it's about time you did," Draco shot back. He stabbed a finger in the direction of the door. "Excuse us. Please." He nearly choked on that final word, before switching his attention to Shayla. She'd run if given half the chance, though considering the extent of her pregnancy he had a reasonable shot at catching her this time round. And it wouldn't take nine months, either. "Shayla and I have a lot to talk about."

Leticia didn't want to leave, he could see the resistance in every line of her whip-thin body. "Very well, I'll go." Her eyes narrowed on Draco, the soft baby blues bright with malice. "But I'll be back."

"Yeah, that's what all villains say," he muttered.

Shayla must have heard because she glanced out the

window, biting her lip. He wondered if it was to hold back laughter or to keep herself from tearing him a new one. The door closed behind Leticia, just shy of a slam, leaving them in murky silence. Draco didn't hesitate. Most of his questions could be answered with one easy move.

Before she realized his intent, he swept her into his arms and kissed her. It was a hard, ruthless kiss, one that gave no quarter, but demanded a response, a definitive answer to months' worth of questions. He put every bit of the loss and hunger, anger and pain, hope and despair into that melding of lips.

He felt her resistance, her initial panic. Her hands pressed against his chest, attempting to hold him at bay. And then it all changed. A soft moan caught in her throat, a moan of intense longing and desire. Where before her hands pushed, now they lifted and tangled in his hair. Tugged to bring him closer. Her lips parted and she deepened the kiss, easing it from hard to generous, ruthless to eager, filling it with a joyful welcome.

She felt good in his arms. Right. Her scent swirled around him, a uniquely familiar one that he connected with on some deep, primal level. And her taste... Her sweet taste and fervent touch caused The Inferno to burn with a blistering intensity. She was his. Had been his from the moment they touched.

A soft kick impacted against his abdomen, coming from the tight mound of Shayla's belly. He broke off the embrace and took a swift step back, staring in shock. "Are you all right? The baby? I think I hurt it."

"Not at all." She smiled, a soft, radiant smile that knocked first at his heart, then at his legs, threatening to send him straight to his knees. "He or she must have felt left out and given you a little kick to say hello."

Draco closed his eyes in relief. Great. *Great way to start, Dante.* He hesitated, not quite certain how to go from there.

He wasn't accustomed to being indecisive and it irritated him. Okay, fine. The hell with starting out by getting his feet wet. He'd just dive right in.

Dragging in a deep breath, he pinned Shayla with his gaze. "Is the baby mine?"

"Are you married?" she countered. "You never actually said. Earlier, I mean."

"No. I'm not married."

"Engaged?" she persisted.

He ran a hand through his hair, reaching deep for the patience he'd lost eight-plus endless months ago. "I'm not married. Not engaged. Not seeing anyone. Not interested in seeing anyone," he asserted. "With one exception. You."

An emotion swept across her elegant features, so fast he couldn't quite identify it. Hurt, maybe? "Then why have you waited so long to come and see me?"

Okay, definitely hurt. He approached, deliberately stepping into a bright patch of sunlight. It cut hot and sharp across his face, giving her a clear view of both his expression and his eyes. "Let me make this crystal clear. I have been searching for you since the moment you disappeared. When you didn't show up for dinner, I stopped by the Mark—who, incidentally had never heard of you. Next, I called your grandmother—who professed ignorance. I won't bother to comment on that."

This time Shayla allowed the smallest of smiles to curve her mouth before bringing it under swift control. "Since I was on a plane, technically she didn't know my precise location."

"If you say so." They'd discuss her departure from San Francisco soon enough. Guaranteed, it would be long and unpleasant. But it would happen. "My third call was to Juice."

Her brow wrinkled in bewilderment. "Who's Juice?"

"He worked for my brother's security firm years ago and after the business closed down, he went independent. Let's just say he's an expert at finding what's lost and recovering it."

Shayla stilled. "You asked him to recover me?" she asked.

"Hell, yes, I asked him to recover you."

She crossed to a window seat overlooking the expansive grounds at the rear of the mansion. Taking a seat, her restless hands folded and refolded the blankets she held. They were handmade baby blankets Draco now realized. "He must not be very good at his job if it took him all this time to find me."

Not quite knowing what to do with himself, Draco paced in front of her. "Maybe if you hadn't spent most of that time trying to dodge me, he'd have had an easier time of it."

"I wasn't dodging you," she corrected. "I had a job that involved extensive travel."

"Yeah, right." He didn't bother to conceal his skepticism. "Regardless, Juice tracked you all over Europe. Maybe if your employer, Algier, weren't such a recluse who keeps his schedule top secret, I would have managed to catch you. I almost pulled it off in Copenhagen." Disgust ripped through his voice. "We probably passed each other at the airport. After that, you fell off the grid."

"I came home," she said simply.

"That was three months ago." Three months. Three impossibly long months and she'd been here all along. Son of a— "I've called your grandmother weekly since you left me high and dry in San Francisco, asking whether you'd been in touch. She categorically denied being in contact with you."

Shayla lifted a shoulder in a shrug that caused her dress to swirl across the surface of her rounded belly. More than anything he wanted to touch her burgeoning flesh, to feel again the impatient kick of the baby tucked safe within her womb. "I asked her not to."

"Got it." A wintry bitterness descended. More and more it would seem Lazz was right. "Was seducing me part of your grandmother's plan in order to gather inside information on the Dantes?"

She froze. "Is that what you think?"

His temper escaped his grasp. "What the hell am I supposed to think, Shayla? We spent one incredible night together. You acted as though it meant as much to you as it did to me. But it was all a lie, wasn't it? You made a date with me, planning all the while to stand me up. You left without a word of explanation, not so much as a note or phone call. Then you went abroad with Derek Algier. Personally, I think you were running like you had the devil at your heels." He allowed nine months of fury to underscore his words. "And you would have been right. I was behind you almost every step of the way, hell-bound to find you."

Other than a telltale trace of color sweeping across her cheekbones, she remained remarkably composed. "If you found out I worked for Derek, then you must know I wasn't running from you."

"I think that job turned out to be a very convenient way of avoiding me." He cut her off before she could slam him with a heated reply. "And if it wasn't, why else would you keep running?" He tried to keep the bite out of the question and failed miserably. "Why else would you have kept your pregnancy a secret?"

"Because you're married."

It took every ounce of self-control not to roar like his namesake. "For the last time, I am *not* married."

"Well, no. But I thought you were." She sighed. "I'll have

to remember to check my facts when it comes to my grand-mother."

"How many years have you known her, and you're only just now coming to that conclusion?" He waved that aside. "Never mind. Answer me this, Shayla. What would you have done if you'd been told the truth from the start? If that—" He swallowed the epithet he was about to use to describe Leticia so he wouldn't offend Shayla. It went down like a bitter pill. "If your grandmother hadn't lied and told you I was married, what would you have done?"

She fell silent for an endless moment. With the light at her back, he couldn't read the expression in her dark eyes. Couldn't tell what she thought or how she felt, and it was killing him inch by torturous inch. Finally, she spoke. "I would have called you to tell you I was pregnant with your baby."

The simple statement hit like a blow to the solar plexus. It took endless seconds to regain use of his lungs and limbs. Once he had, he approached and sank onto the padded bench beside her. The sunshine streamed in through the window and warmed his back like a blessing. Ever so gently he reached out and slid his hand across her abdomen. The Inferno burned hot against his palm, hot against the life cupped beneath.

"Our baby," he murmured.

To his surprise, Shayla leaned into him and allowed her head to fall against his shoulder. It struck him that if he'd been wrong about his suspicions—that going to bed with him had not been part of some Machiavellian plot forged by Leticia Charleston—then Shayla had probably spent the past nine months standing strong, all on her own. Granted, she had the Wicked Witch to assist her, but that couldn't have been much help. Not when her grandmother had a hidden agenda she was clearly running, play by dangerous play.

The best he could tell, there were two options. Either

Leticia and Shayla had devised a plan of revenge to even the score with the Dantes for long-past transgressions, and sleeping with him was somehow part of it. Or Shayla was an innocent bystander. He was absolutely certain about one thing. Leticia was up to something. The Dantes just hadn't uncovered the how-and-when portion of the slowly unfolding play. But guaranteed, the instant the curtain fell on the final act, it would be with a dagger in their collective backs.

It was also clear to him that Leticia wanted to keep him well away from Shayla and their baby. The question was...why? Was the baby somehow part of her plot, or an unexpected wrinkle? And how much did Shayla know? How involved was she in all this? Only time would tell. Until then, first things first.

"Why would your grandmother go out of her way to keep us apart?" he demanded. "Wouldn't she want the baby to have a name?"

Shayla stiffened. "The baby will have a name. My name. The Charleston name."

"Our baby is a Dante," he corrected implacably. "He'll have the Dante name. We'll marry as soon as it can be arranged."

Where some women would have gotten angry and obstinate, Shayla simply smiled. "You can't force me to the altar, Draco. I've lived almost my entire life with Grandmother Charleston. She's spent the past seventy-two years learning how to operate a steamroller and she's one of the best at it I've ever seen. I've lived my entire life sidestepping her. If she can't force me in the direction she wants me to go, what makes you think you'll have any better success?"

Shayla was like moonbeams and stardust, filled with magic but impossible to pin down. But that didn't mean he wouldn't try. "Because you want what's best for our child. And staying here, raising a child as a single mother, having your grandmother as a strong influence in your baby's life is not in our child's best interest."

"But you are?"

"I'm his father," Draco stated simply.

"His?" she repeated.

"Chances are it's a boy. The Dantes have never quite gotten the hang of producing daughters, despite the occasional error in judgment." He grinned to let her know he was teasing about his sister, Gianna. "Regardless of the sex, I intend to be there for our child on a daily basis. Not for the occasional, flying visit, but every single day of his or her life."

"I see."

She appeared troubled, which disturbed him more than he cared to admit. After all, what had she expected him to say? "Good luck and goodbye"? Or... "Here's the monthly check, don't call me, I'll call you"? He tilted his head to one side. "You have a problem with my being involved?"

"Not exactly."

He pushed. "Then what exactly?"

She fussed with the blankets some more, though the best he could tell they weren't going to fold any neater. "I gather that this daily contact is supposed to take place in San Francisco?"

"I'd be willing to move here," he conceded. "But there's another important point you should take into consideration before deciding where we live. If you and the baby join me in San Francisco, you'll both be surrounded by the love and support of my family. Our son will have grandparents who'll adore him and be an intricate part of his life. And he'll have more aunts and uncles and cousins than he can count."

"I grew up without all of that," she countered. "I've done just fine."

That was open to debate. Fortunately, he retained sufficient discretion not to point that out. "The Dantes all get together

at least once a week at Primo's. We vacation together during
the summer at our lake house. The wives all support each
other and help with babysitting duties. Granted, considering
your background you may find all the intermingling a bit
overwhelming at first, everybody in everybody else's business.
But would you deny our son the opportunity to be part of
such a large, close-knit family? Be honest, Shayla. Didn't you
miss that growing up? Which is the better lifestyle, here or
there?"

"If I decide that moving to San Francisco is a better
option, why does it have to involve marriage?" she asked in
a reasonable voice. "Marriage is a huge commitment. And
it's not like we're in love with each other."

He forced himself to remain silent, to choose his words as
though they were the most precious of commodities. "I come
from an old-world, extremely traditional Italian family, one
in which premarital sex doesn't happen."

She blinked. "Then what did we have?"

He smiled. "Premarital sex." His smile faded. "But for my
grandparents it doesn't exist, and therefore, didn't happen."

"Boy, are they going to be in for a surprise in a couple
weeks," she murmured.

He didn't want to think about that, couldn't be distracted
by it. But he wanted her to understand who he was and where
he'd come from. "If you were to have our baby outside of
wedlock, I would shame Primo and Nonna because I didn't
marry you and provide our son with the Dante name. They
would never get over it."

Distress filled her eyes, turning them black as midnight.
"They'd disown you, wouldn't they?"

"Once upon a time, perhaps, when the line was blacker and
more rigidly drawn. But they lost their son and daughter-in-
law—my uncle and his wife—in a sailing accident. It changed
my grandparents, made them hold tighter to those of us who

were left. So, no. They wouldn't disown me. Even if that were a possibility, I wouldn't try to force you to marry me because of it."

"But your relationship with them will never be the same if I don't marry you." When he remained silent, she pressed. "Will it?"

He hadn't expected her to be so shrewd. "It would change," he conceded.

"And if we married? Even if it's only weeks before our baby is born?"

"I'd make it clear that I moved heaven and earth these past months searching for you, intent on finding and marrying you. That even if I'd known you were pregnant I couldn't have done any more in order to track you down. I'll also make it clear that you didn't contact me because you were operating under the mistaken impression that I was already married. Primo would have words with me, no question there. But since you and the baby would bear the Dante name, it would go a long way toward smoothing everything over."

"Why, Draco?" she asked in bewilderment. "Why have you been looking for me all this time?"

"You know why."

He laced her hand with his, pressing palm against palm, Inferno against Inferno. He watched her weigh the options, watched while his entire future hung in the balance. She almost tipped, when suddenly she grimaced. She slipped her hand from his to rest it low on her back and press, the gesture one of supreme weariness. He'd been around enough pregnant women in recent months to understand the source of her discomfort and take a fairly accurate stab at how to relieve it.

"Let me help," he offered.

Gently he shifted her on the window seat so he could get to her back. Running his hands down her spine, he cautiously pressed until he found the bundle of knots just above her buttocks. Then he sank the heel of his palm into the source of her pain and worked at it. Her low moan had him clenching, building a number of knots of his own to replace the ones he relieved in her back.

"How did you learn to do that?" she marveled.

"Watching my cousins and brothers with their wives."

He rested his jaw alongside her temple. He wished he could sit like this for hours, absorbing the soft texture of her skin against his, inhaling her sweet scent with each breath he took, feeling the quiet joy of having her in his arms. He didn't care what it required or what sacrifices he needed to make. This woman was his and he refused to let her go. Not again. Not ever.

"Shayla…"

She stiffened, pulled away from him. "Don't pressure me, Draco. I'm not going to marry you because I'm pregnant with our child, or because of Primo and Nonna, or even for Alessandro and Elia." The use of his parents' names had him shooting her a questioning look. "I've made a point of acquiring a genealogy of your family," she explained.

"Why?"

"Because the baby will need to know who his family is." Her response registered on some deep, elemental level, but before he could comment, she continued. "I can't make any decisions until I speak to Grandmother Charleston. I want to know why she told me you were married."

He could take several wild guesses, but kept them to himself. At least, for now. It wouldn't help his cause to go after Shayla's sole remaining family member. A hideous thought occurred to him and he closed his eyes, wincing. Hell. If he and Shayla married, he'd be related to the old bat through marriage. She'd be his grandmonster-in-law.

And the hits just kept on coming.

As though waiting for her cue to return, Leticia swept into the room and shot off her opening volley. "If you've settled your business with my granddaughter, Mr. Dante, you may feel free to vacate my home."

Draco folded his arms across his chest. "I'm not leaving without Shayla."

"We'll just see about that. One phone call and I can have you removed, by force if necessary. My second phone call will be to my lawyer telling him to tear up the contract authorizing the sale of the Charleston mines to your family."

Shayla waded into the fray. "If everyone is finished making idle threats, we all have some decisions to make."

Leticia sat down abruptly. "I can't begin to imagine what you're talking about. What decisions?"

"For one, whether or not I'm going to marry Draco and move to San Francisco with him."

The words were barely out of Shayla's mouth before Leticia shot to her feet again. "I forbid it! I absolutely, unequivocally forbid it."

Draco was so grateful, he was tempted to kiss the hideous old woman on her narrow, cotton candy-pink mouth. She couldn't have picked a worse comment to make if she'd tried, or one more guaranteed to drive her granddaughter in the exact opposite direction of the one she wanted.

Sure enough, Shayla's eyes narrowed. "You forbid?" she repeated softly.

Draco had to hand it to her. Despite her advanced years, the old broad could still do a fast backtrack. "Perhaps the word *forbid* was ill-advised," she graciously conceded. "But, darling, you must think about what's best for the baby. And flying in your condition could prove dangerous. I'm certain your obstetrician would never agree to it. I suggest you wait until after the baby is born. Then you can go out and visit the Dantes with your—" she lifted her eyes heavenward, a pained expression painted across her face "—little bundle of joy."

It was the look that must have decided Shayla, a look that warned that Leticia Charleston would never forgive her granddaughter for having the temerity to give birth to a child half Dante. It also provided answers to several of Draco's questions, such as whether or not sleeping with him was part of a Charleston plot. Clearly, it wasn't.

Shayla turned to Draco, the pain in her gaze threatening to rip him apart. Though he rejoiced that Leticia had tipped the scales in his favor, he hated that she'd hurt Shayla in the process.

"When can we leave?" she whispered, her breath catching in a slight hiccup.

"That depends. How fast can you pack?"

"Wait!" Leticia aimed for entreaty and still hit demand. "Please, wait, Shayla. I don't want you to leave."

"I understand, Grandmother," she replied gently. "But you've said it yourself. I have to do what's best for my baby."

"But you're the last Charleston in our family. You could have a son." Leticia directed a fulminating glare at Draco. "Dantes have a history of shooting out sons like gumballs from a nickel machine. If you had a boy, he'd be a Charleston. Our name, our line, would continue."

Shayla gasped in disbelief. "Is *that* why you told me Draco was married? Why you worked so hard to keep him from finding me and discovering I was pregnant? So I'd produce a Charleston heir?"

Leticia lifted a shoulder, somehow managing to imbue the gesture with a wealth of exasperation. "That might be one of the reasons on my list. It's not the first item, but it's on there, somewhere. I don't normally approve of illegitimacy, although considering the current benefits to our line, I am willing to make a one-time exception. Even if the boy will be half Dante."

"Very gracious of you," Draco said carefully.

She turned on him like the viper she was. "Oh, get over it," she snapped. "You found out in the nick of time, didn't you? You Dantes always find a way to win the day. So, go ahead and fly her out to California. Your family probably owns a fleet of private planes. Wave your hand and make one of them appear. With any luck the flight will force her into premature labor before you can drag her to the altar. And I'll still get my way…assuming the baby survives."

"Why, you—"

"That's enough." Shayla never raised her voice, yet sheer steel shot through her words, making them all the more powerful. "Grandmother has a point. Before I leave I should visit Dr. Dorling and have him determine the best way for us to get to California." She fixed her grandmother with an unyielding stare. "But I am leaving. I will do what's best for my baby and right now that's Draco."

"And if I refuse to sell the Dantes our mine?" Leticia stalked in Draco's direction though she was smart enough to stay well out of his reach. She gripped her wedding ring, tugging at the chain so hard he wondered if it would snap. "If I threaten to sell it to one of your competitors if you marry my granddaughter? What then?"

There was only one response to her threat, a response— given the circumstances—Draco couldn't resist using. "Frankly, my dear, I don't give a damn."

Five

"How are you feeling?"

Shayla sighed. It must have been at least the twentieth time Draco had asked that question. From the moment they went wheels up, he'd watched her with all the ferocity of a fire-breathing dragon, as though he were guarding a treasure more precious than gold.

"I'm fine," she assured both him and Dr. Dorling. How Draco had convinced her obstetrician to join them on the flight, she had no idea. No doubt it involved a sizable amount of money since the doctor had dropped everything to make the trip. "I feel great."

Dr. Dorling checked the monitors and nodded toward Draco. "Everything is perfect, Mr. Dante. Good oxygen. Excellent heart rate for both mother and baby. Blood pressure right where it should be."

Draco didn't appear the least relieved. Though he didn't pace, Shayla could feel his worry electrifying the space within the luxurious confines of the Dantes' jet. "We should arrive in another two hours," he muttered, digging his thumb into his palm. His Infernoed palm, she noted. "Not long now."

"Draco..."

"It's all right, sweetheart," he attempted to soothe in a voice overflowing with grit and tension. "The pilot has the coordinates for all the landing strips close to hospitals along our flight path."

"Draco." She waited until he gave her his undivided attention. "Would you please relax? The flight isn't making me nervous. The baby isn't making me nervous. The doctor and his machines aren't making me nervous. *You* are."

He blew out a sigh, then smiled, two deep grooves denting his cheeks. It was the smile that did her in. But then, it was his smile that had coaxed her into his bed in the first place. His smile. The burn of his touch. That odd sizzle and jolt when they'd first touched, a sensation that refused to go away, even after more than nine impossibly long months.

He crossed to join her, sliding in beside her and tucking her close. She closed her eyes, absorbing his warmth and allowing the steady beat of his heart and quiet movement of air in and out of his lungs to lull her toward a peaceful limbo. These days she lived in a haze of exhaustion, not to mention feeling uncomfortable and awkward, able to nap at any given moment, though with the constant kicks from the baby, never for long. Her life had changed in monumental ways, and all because of the man who held her safe and secure within his arms.

Years before she'd formulated a plan for her life, one she finally implemented during her stay in San Francisco. She'd been so excited beforehand, seen the possibilities so clearly, without anticipating how her impulsive actions the night she met Draco would ultimately change her life. That had been brought home during those first two months in Europe when her longing for him had been keen and sharp. Months during which pain and loss outweighed the thrill of achieving her ideal job.

Oh, she loved translating for Derek. Adored her employer, one of the kindest, most understanding men she'd ever met. When she'd realized she was pregnant, he'd kept her on as long as he could. But eventually the whispers and suspicion that he'd fathered her baby had interfered with his business negotiations. Plus, the first five months of her pregnancy had been rough, her morning sickness closer to all-day sickness. Finally, she'd decided it simply wasn't safe or healthy to be globe-trotting around Europe during her pregnancy. So, she'd returned home.

She refused to regret the sharp turn her life had taken thanks to that one night with Draco. Regrets weren't part of her nature. And now, once again due to the man who held her so securely in his arms, her life was about to take another acute turn, one she didn't think she could handle.

Draco tucked a lock of her hair behind her ear and she shivered at the touch. "What are you thinking about?" he murmured close to her ear.

"About what will happen when we reach San Francisco," she replied readily enough.

"Nothing very dramatic. I'll take you home once Dr. Dorling is satisfied that you're stable. And then you'll rest."

She made a face. "That's not what I meant."

"We can discuss any other concerns tonight. There's no hurry."

"Yes, there is and you know it." She rubbed her belly, felt the tautness. Knew the baby had dropped low in her womb, eager to escape the safety of its nest. "This cake is just about baked."

She felt his chuckle against her cheek. "Did you just call our baby a cake?"

A reluctant laugh sighed from her. "I guess I did."

He bent down and kissed her. Maybe if the kiss had been like before, hard and hungry and filled with a desperate edge, she'd have been able to resist. But it wasn't. He soothed her with his taking, calmed her with gentleness, roused her with tenderness, branded her with a kiss that caused all others to pale in comparison.

"Well, that got her heart rate and blood pressure up," Dr. Dorling observed. "You might want to save that until after we land."

Reluctantly, Draco pulled back. His tawny eyes glittered like antique gold, filled with a want that echoed her own. "You think there's a lot we need to resolve," he told her in an intimate undertone, low enough that the doctor couldn't overhear. "But that kiss tells me there isn't as much to discuss as you might think."

When she opened her mouth to argue, he shook his head. "Close your eyes, Shayla. Let go and sleep. We'll worry about the future later."

"We?" she murmured.

Naturally, he got the last word, something that she was beginning to realize he excelled at. "Since it's our future, it concerns the both of us."

The quiet beep of the machines joined in tempo with the reassuring beat of Draco's heart. It proved the perfect sedative, sending her off into an easy sleep filled with the most romantic of dreams about a dragon and a princess and sweet rescue. But it vanished like fairy dust the instant the pitch of the jet engines changed. She opened her eyes, blinking in confusion.

"We're starting our descent," Draco informed her. "We should be home in a little over an hour, depending on traffic."

Home.

She assumed he meant his home and wondered how she'd

feel about staying there. Like a guest? Like an intruder? She'd wanted her own place for more years than she could count, a nest she could burrow into and feather with the bits and pieces that would make it distinctly hers. Now that possibility grew less and less likely.

The minute they touched down at a small regional airport outside of the city, Dr. Dorling gave her a final examination. As soon as he cleared her, she thanked him for all his time and assistance. He gave her the name of a colleague who agreed to take over her care from this point forward and was expecting her visit bright and early the next morning.

Draco handed the obstetrician a first-class ticket that would return him to Atlanta on a commercial flight and they all exited the plane. While the doctor headed off to San Francisco International Airport in one car, another car, complete with driver, awaited to take them home—wherever that was.

"Sausalito," Draco said, as though reading her mind. "Not far from Primo and Nonna."

"I thought you lived in the suite where we—"

She broke off abruptly. Where they'd made love. Where she'd conceived their child, though she hadn't known it at the time. Where she'd created a connection that continued even after all this time, gaining in strength with each passing day. But she couldn't say any of those things aloud, not when the driver might overhear them.

"I don't live at the suite," he explained. "I just stayed at Dantes while my house was under construction. The designer put the last few touches on the place yesterday, so I haven't seen the final product." He smiled at her. "We'll get to do that together."

"I'll enjoy that." She hesitated. "Do they know about me?" she whispered, sparing the driver another uneasy glance.

Draco must have picked up on her concern because he leaned forward to give the driver directions to his house, then engaged the privacy screen. "It's soundproof," he reassured before picking up the conversational thread again. "I assume you mean, does my family know about you? No, not yet. I didn't want to say anything until we've had time to discuss our options and make decisions about the future."

"I guess you won't be able to keep me hidden for long." She touched her belly to include the existence of their baby. "Not if your family is as close-knit as you say."

He appeared remarkably unconcerned. "I'm hoping it won't take us long to decide what's best for the three of us."

"You think that's marriage." No question there. He'd made that fact abundantly clear.

He lifted a shoulder in a casual shrug. "What can I say? It's how I was raised."

She glanced out the tinted window. She couldn't argue the point. It was how she'd been raised, too. "There's one serious problem with your plan."

"Name it and I'll see if I can't solve it," he replied promptly.

"Solve it," she repeated. She swiveled to face him. "Fixing problems. Finding a way to make sure the roadblocks are removed so you can get from Point A to Point B. That's a core part of your personality, isn't it?"

He didn't deny it. "It's one aspect, yes. I also protect what's mine and do whatever is necessary to recover what's taken from me, whether that takes months…" A darkness flitted through his gaze. "Or years."

She shivered, his expression shooting a chill of dread down her spine. "Is that what I am to you? A possession to be recovered?"

His voice deepened, roughened. "Recovering you is like

recovering a missing piece of myself. Without you, I'm empty. And I suspect you are, as well."

Her throat closed over and she stared at him mutely.

He cupped her face and feathered a kiss across her mouth. "More important, I'll do everything within my power to protect you and our baby. To protect you, provide for you, to try to make you happy."

Shayla snatched a deep breath. "And what about the roadblocks that are in our way?" To her relief, her voice sounded fairly normal, not revealing a trace of the hunger and longing that shot through her.

"What roadblocks?"

"Marriage, for one." She steeled herself, then gave it to him straight. "How do you clear the roadblocks so that we fall in love with each other? Because that's the only reason I'll marry you."

He froze, every scrap of emotion wiped from his expression. He didn't reply. He simply reached for her hand and interlaced it with his, allowing The Inferno to speak for him. And speak it did.

The want roared through her, blistering hot and filled with urgent demand. It didn't matter that she was heavy with his child or that they'd been parted since last summer. Whatever connected them, whether lust or something more, something she couldn't bring herself to recognize, it hadn't dimmed over time. She longed for him on every level, felt the tug at her heart and fought against the emotions that threatened to entrap it. Whatever this feeling, it wasn't love. After so short a time together that would be impossible.

"It's just physical," she insisted beneath her breath. "It isn't real."

"It's a start," Draco replied implacably. "For the sake of our child, we should give it a chance."

She closed her eyes, exhaustion and worry sapping her energy. "You don't understand."

"Then explain it to me."

She hated to strip bare the more painful details of her life, to allow someone to poke and prod indiscriminately at what she preferred to keep private. But Draco deserved that much. She focused on him, her emotions seeping free of her self-control.

"You've met my grandmother, so you can probably imagine how long and hard I've had to fight just to maintain my own identity, to keep from turning into her image of who Shayla Charleston should be."

"It must have been difficult for you."

She could see the bitter comments piling up behind that single, curt observation and appreciated his restraint. "Almost impossible," she confirmed. "I couldn't give an inch or she'd take the proverbial mile."

"Sounds like Leticia."

"Yes, well…" She twisted her hands together. "I lived at home while attending college. It wasn't ideal since my grandmother knew my schedule and expected me to adhere to it."

To her relief, he read between the lines. It wouldn't have been difficult considering she'd been a virgin when he took her to his bed. "I imagine that had a serious impact on your social life."

"I had no social life," she admitted. "Living at home—or rather, with my grandmother—prevented me from enjoying the full college experience."

"Then why do it that way?"

Shayla shrugged. "Because it was cheaper," she said simply. "As a result, I formulated a series of goals for my future that helped get me through college. I couldn't implement them right away, but at least I had them. They were like shiny

Christmas presents waiting for the right time and place to be unwrapped."

He regarded her curiously. "Why couldn't you unwrap them right away?"

Shayla sighed. "Grandmother spent the last of her money on sending me to college. She had dreams of her own. Dreams for rebuilding Charlestons and our chain of jewelry stores. I don't know how she planned to finance it, since she hadn't discovered the fire diamonds at that point. But I was supposed to run the business."

"I gather that didn't appeal to you?"

She shook her head. "That wasn't the real issue. After everything she'd done for me, I'd have stepped up. I took the courses she requested so I'd know enough to tell a good stone from a bad and recognize a fake. Accounting and business courses, as well. But, I don't have the temperament for either, let alone management. And I have zero artistic flare. In other words, I'd be utterly useless helping to rebuild Charlestons. We'd have only ended up bankrupt again. It took a long time before my grandmother came to terms with that fact. To be honest, I'm not fully convinced she has even now."

"What did you want to do instead?"

"I have a natural facility for languages, along with a desire to see other countries and experience their cultures. So, I made a trade with Grandmother. For every course she wanted me to take, I enrolled in one I wanted. My ultimate dream has always been to get a job overseas as a translator."

"That would have taken you out from under Leticia's thumb." Draco pinpointed the problem with typical perceptiveness. "I assume she didn't react well to the idea?"

"She exploded when I told her." Shayla shrugged. "I can understand. After all, there's only the two of us left. Considering everything she's been through, it made it all the more imperative that I find a way to support us. She just objected to how I chose to go about it."

His eyes narrowed. "Knowing your grandmother, she must have found a way to bring pressure to bear. Trowel on the guilt, good and thick." He tilted his head to one side, analyzing, then smiled grimly. "She paid for your education. Used every last dime to her name. She'd lose the mansion if you didn't succeed as a translator. How am I doing so far? Close?"

"You are really good," Shayla marveled. "That's exactly what she said. So I spent the next three years working nonstop in order to pay her back. And I postponed my own plans. When she announced that our diamond mines weren't depleted after all, that a surveyor had not only discovered more, but even better, they contained fire diamonds, I saw my opportunity to pursue the career I always wanted."

"A serious miscalculation on Leticia's part. That's not like her."

Shayla smiled. "She did raise the idea of reopening Charlestons with me once again until I forced her to accept the futility of her plan. I'm simply not competent to run the business. Approaching Dantes was the compromise. It would provide her with the money to revitalize the mansion and keep her comfortable for her remaining years. And it would allow me to find the job of my dreams, which I promptly did."

"All of this went down before we met?"

Shayla nodded. "I updated my passport and applied for a number of positions that offered travel abroad. I was thrilled when the one I wanted the most panned out. Derek needed someone who could leave the country almost immediately. I told my grandmother about it right before I boarded the plane for San Francisco."

"When were you scheduled to leave the country?" he asked in a neutral voice.

She forced herself to meet his gaze, even though she'd have preferred to look anywhere but. "The same evening as our date."

"Why?" He ground out the question, anger reverberating through that single word.

She didn't prevaricate, but told him the truth. "Because I didn't want you to try to stop me."

"Could I have?"

Lord, give her strength. She closed her eyes against the demand in his. Could he have stopped her? Without question. All it would have taken was a single kiss. Kiss? A single look. A single touch, Inferno to Inferno. When it came to Draco Dante, she had zero self-control.

He was waiting for her response and she gathered herself sufficiently to give it to him. "Suffice to say, I wasn't willing to risk the possibility," she replied, neatly sidestepping the issue. "By the time you realized I was gone, I'd be on my way to Barcelona with Derek." He wouldn't like this other part, either. "There's more."

He grimaced. "Might as well put it all out there."

She twisted her hands together, aware that when she finished he wouldn't press for marriage any longer. In fact, she'd be lucky if he didn't just pitch her out of the car, altogether. "My plan contained three parts, goals I wanted to achieve before I turned twenty-five. The first was to find the job of my dreams."

"Enter Derek. Check."

"The second was to provide for my grandmother by offering your family the lease to our mines."

"Meet with the Dantes. Double check." His eyes narrowed, amber hard. "And the third?"

"I turned twenty-five the morning after we met," she began

before trailing off. She wanted to just say it, to get it out there and over with, but she found that she couldn't. Her breath escaped in a slow sigh.

It only took Draco a moment to catch on. "*That's* why you slept with me?" Outrage underscored the question. "You planned to lose your virginity before you turned twenty-five?"

She shook her head. "No!" She flinched. "Well, yes. But not the way you think."

"And I was the lucky guy you chose?"

Did he have to make it sound so lurid? "You don't understand," she tried again. "It wasn't about losing my virginity." How did she explain? "I wanted, just once, to experience a wild, passionate affair. To be swept off my feet and have a single night of pure romance."

"In other words, it could have been any man at the reception that night, even one of my relatives. I was simply the luck of the draw." A muscle leaped along his jaw, warning that he held on to his temper by a mere thread. "It had nothing to do with The Inferno or who I was as a person. You just wanted to sleep with someone before jetting off with good ol' Derek."

A wave of humiliation sent heat streaking across her cheeks while tears pricked her eyes. She fought them back, fought for composure. During the planning stages, having a one-night stand had sounded intrepid, romantic even. Something so out-of-character that she hadn't dared consider it while living in her grandmother's home. Unfortunately, she'd become the poster child for the consequences of illicit sex, even with protection. They might as well slap a photo of her, along with her giant belly, on all the high school walls in the country as a warning. *This could be you!*

"To be fair, I don't think you were too concerned about

who I was as a person, either," she pointed out. "Not at first."

"In other words, if you'd known I was a Dante beforehand, you'd have tumbled into some other man's bed that night."

The tears she'd been holding back through sheer force of will overflowed. "I'm sorry. I don't know what else to say. I wanted to be honest with you so you'd understand why marriage is out of the question. You don't love me anymore than I love you."

He swore. "Don't cry. Please, don't cry, Shayla. It can't be good for either you or the baby."

"I'm not a damn water tap," she managed to protest through her tears. "It's not like I can turn it off with a twist of a knob."

For some reason that made his mouth twitch and a second later she was laughing and crying all at the same time. He opened her purse, found a packet of tissues and pulled one out. He dabbed at her cheeks and eyes and nose.

"Listen to me, sweetheart," he said. "You're tired. I'm tired. We probably could have picked a better time for this conversation."

"I needed to be honest with you."

"I got that. Maybe all that honesty should have come at a slower pace and after a good night's sleep." He gave it further consideration. "And maybe accompanied by several shots of Johnnie Walker."

"Okay." She leaned back against the leather seat and closed her eyes. Exhaustion rolled across her like fog across the bay. "I'm trying, Draco. I've moved out here so our baby will be close to you and the rest of the Dantes. But that's as far as I'm willing to go. I'm not sure I can handle marriage on top of everything else."

"Why?" The question exploded from him, hanging in the air.

It took an unbelievable amount of effort just to open a single eye. "I don't suppose there's any Johnnie Walker stashed in here somewhere?"

"Am I going to need it?"

"Probably."

"Hell." He gave an irritable shrug. "You might as well get it all out. I can't deal with it if I don't know what the problem is."

"That's what you said last time," she muttered.

"Go on. Hit me."

"Okay, here it is… I worked for four long years to carve out the sort of life I wanted. It only took me one night to put an end to that dream." She splayed her hand across her extended abdomen, gave it a gentle rub. "Don't misunderstand. I'll love our baby. I'll never regret having him." She shook her head in exasperation. "*Him?* Now you have me doing it."

"Trust me. It's going to be a boy."

"Fine." She dismissed that with a flick of her fingers. "The point is… Those few months abroad were the best of my life. I was unchained and independent. Until then, I'd never experienced that level of freedom before. Now you want me to marry you. To move in with you. To forcibly create a family. It's going to be tough enough that I'm here in a strange city with a newborn. I'm not sure I can handle marriage on top of everything else. To be honest, I don't want to lose any more of my independence."

Draco was silent for a long time and she wondered if she'd offended him again. "You don't have to handle marriage," he finally said. "There's another option."

Hope blossomed. "What option?"

"We'll make a premarital agreement…a marriage pact, if that works for you. We marry to give the baby the Dante name, but we don't have to live together, if you'd rather not." She caught a certain grimness in his voice, a stoic quality that disturbed her. "It'll be your choice. If and when you want a real marriage, we can reconsider that possibility."

"You'd be willing to do that?" she asked in surprise. "Wouldn't your family notice?"

"It's none of their business."

She gave a short laugh. "That might be your opinion and it might be mine, as well, but I've discovered that it's never the opinion of the rest of the family. They always think they have the right to interfere."

"There's only one person's opinion that matters to me and that's yours. As for my family… Don't worry about them. I'll keep them off your back."

She could feel herself softening. She probably should have insisted on revisiting the discussion in the morning when she'd had time to rest and consider. But instead, she found herself nodding. "Okay, I agree."

He stilled. "You'll marry me?"

"Yes," she found herself saying. Clearly, she'd lost her mind.

"Tomorrow?"

Her eyebrows winged upward. "Can we get married that fast?"

"Absolutely. I'll make the arrangements as soon as we get home."

Panic built in the pit of her stomach and more than anything she wanted to change her mind. Instead, she nodded. "It's a deal."

He gathered her up in his arms. "Since we can't toast our agreement with champagne, we'll seal the deal with another time-honored tradition."

She had a split second to prepare herself before he lowered his head and kissed her, kissed her with a thoroughness that drove every other thought from her head. Their kiss yesterday had been filled with hunger and demand. The one on the plane a gentle benediction. This one was sheer temptation, as though he were reminding her of that wonderfully illicit evening nine months ago when passion had ruled the night and she'd unknowingly surrendered to the ultimate temptation.

Now Draco's kiss stormed her senses, making her forget everything but this man and this moment. For a brief instant she even forgot the baby tucked safely beneath her heart, a baby who'd been the result of that surrender. A baby born from passion and who would know the love of both parents, as well as countless family members.

For her baby's sake, marrying Draco was the smart choice. The only choice. But for her own sake…?

Before she could consider the question, he reluctantly released her and glanced outside. Shayla suddenly realized they'd arrived. While the driver unloaded their bags, Draco helped her from the car, a process that became more difficult with each passing day. A tip passed from his hand to the chauffer's and then they were alone.

She took a moment to study his home while she attempted to unknot the muscles in her back. The house stood wide and proud, a stunning multilevel wood-and-glass structure perched high on the hillside with an incredible view of the bay.

"It's gorgeous," she murmured.

"Wait until you see the inside."

He guided her along the walkway to the front door, stuck his key in the lock and flung open the door. Gently, carefully, tenderly, he lifted her in his arms and carried her across the threshold. "Welcome home," he said.

At the same moment an endless crowd of people jumped out from doorways and closets and from behind furniture, all shouting, "Surprise!"

The instant they realized Draco wasn't alone, silence descended. All eyes locked on Shayla…or more specifically,

Shayla's belly. Primo stood front and center in the middle of the throng, his golden gaze taking in the situation in a single fierce glance.

"Well," he said after a long, awkward moment. "It would seem the surprise is on us, eh?"

FREE Merchandise is 'in the Cards' for you!

Dear Reader,

We're giving away FREE MERCHANDISE!

Seriously, we'd like to reward you for reading this novel by giving you **FREE MERCHANDISE** worth over **$20**. And no purchase is necessary!

You see the Jack of Hearts sticker above? Paste that sticker in the box on the Free Merchandise Voucher inside. Return the Voucher promptly...and we'll send you valuable Free Merchandise!

Thanks again for reading one of our novels—and enjoy your Free Merchandise with our compliments!

Pam Powers

Pam Powers

P.S. Look inside to see what Free Merchandise is **"in the cards"** for you!

(S-D-12/10)

W

We'd like to send you two free books to introduce you to the Silhouette Desire® series. These books are worth over $10, but they are yours to keep absolutely FREE! We'll even send you 2 wonderful surprise gifts. You can't lose!

REMEMBER: Your Free Merchandise, consisting of **2 Free Books** and **2 Free Gifts**, is worth over $20.00! No purchase is necessary, so please send for your Free Merchandise today.

YOUR FREE MERCHANDISE INCLUDES...

2 FREE Silhouette Desire® Books
AND 2 FREE Mystery Gifts

FREE MERCHANDISE VOUCHER

2 FREE BOOKS and 2 FREE GIFTS

Please send my Free Merchandise, consisting of
2 Free Books and **2 Free Mystery Gifts**.
I understand that I am under no obligation to buy
anything, as explained on the back of this card.

*About how many NEW paperback fiction books
have you purchased in the past 3 months?*

☐ 0-2   ☐ 3-6   ☐ 7 or more
E9FY   E9GC   E9GN

225/326 SDL

Please Print

FIRST NAME

LAST NAME

ADDRESS

APT.#   CITY

STATE/PROV.   ZIP/POSTAL CODE

NO PURCHASE NECESSARY!

Six

Draco watched his wife-to-be take one look at Primo and start babbling. In Italian, no less.

"We're getting married, I swear. First thing in the morning. Well, not first thing. I have a doctor's appointment that I don't think Draco will let me miss. But right after that we're going straight to a justice of the peace and tying the knot. And don't blame your grandson. It's not his fault. He didn't know I was pregnant and he's been looking for me for nine months and would have insisted we marry even if I weren't." She paused long enough to snatch a quick breath. "Pregnant, I mean."

Draco gently eased Shayla onto her feet. "So, what's *your* surprise?" he asked his family.

Primo locked eyes with Draco, a wealth of information passing between them without a single word being spoken. "Your home. It is finished," his grandfather announced at last. "We are giving you a surprise hothouse party. The women, they say it is tradition."

It took Draco a split second to realize that hothouse meant housewarming. "Thank you. I appreciate it. Maybe we can also make it a pre-wedding celebration?"

His gaze swept his relatives, taking in the various reactions ranging from shock to bemusement to out-and-out laughter. Then they closed ranks. After all, they were Dantes and Dantes protected their own. They swept up Shayla, carried her off and eased her onto a couch, building pillows around her for added comfort. One by one, family members approached and introduced themselves while they plied her with food and friendly get-to-know-you questions.

Primo jerked his head toward the outside deck and Draco released a sigh of regret that he wasn't also being pillowed and fed—and wouldn't be anytime in the near future. Once they were outside Primo fumbled in his pocket for the cigar he always carried there, much to Nonna's annoyance, not to mention his physician's. He offered a second to Draco, who knew better than to refuse, given the current circumstances. The two men took their time with the trimming and lighting.

Then Primo devastated Draco with a single look. "You did this to her?"

The words, the look, all had him flinching. "The baby is mine, yes. I'm sorry, Primo. This isn't the way I'd planned things."

"I am unaware of the fact that you plan at all."

The comment stung. Once upon a time it might have been true. But he'd worked long and hard the past decade to prove himself. To overcome the shame of losing the fire diamonds at a time his family teetered on the brink of financial ruin.

Draco fought for patience. "You know The Inferno hit the night of the Eternity reception. And you know Shayla disappeared the next day after we met to discuss leasing the Charleston mines." He paced to the railing and studied the spectacular view through eyes blinded by the past rather than focused on the present. "I've been searching for her ever since she left. Two days ago I finally found her."

"You marry tomorrow?"

"Yes."

"Not by this justice of the peace, *istigatore*."

Draco's mouth tightened. He'd always been considered a troublemaker by his grandfather. Only time would change that. Or maybe, once labeled, it would never change. "How, when and where?"

"I will provide you with the place. My place." Primo stabbed his cigar in Draco's direction. "A small backyard wedding, yes? With the family. And no city official, but a priest. If we can arrange this for tomorrow, *buon*. If not, *presto*. Very soon." He fixed his grandson with a calculating gaze. "My math, it is good. I can add how many months and weeks have slipped by since the reception. The baby, he will not wait much longer."

"No, he won't."

"And your Nonna, she will cry if *il bambino* comes into the world without the Dante name to protect him. You know what I do to any man who makes my *bellezza* weep?" Primo's eyes glittered with threat and promise. "Would you care to guess, *nipote?*"

Draco's mouth settled into grim lines. The same thing he'd do to any man who made Shayla weep. Beat the living crap out of him. "I have a pretty good idea. Trust me, I won't allow that to happen."

"*Buon, buon.*" Primo clapped his hand on Draco's shoulder. "I know you have searched for your Inferno mate these many months. Luc tells me you asked Juice to help find her the very night you lost her. You have done right in this. But you should not have taken her to your bed without first putting your ring on her finger. To do so dishonors the two of you, not to mention your family. You know this now, yes?"

"*Sì*, Primo. *Sono spiacente*," he apologized.

A smoke trail swept in the direction of the relatives clustered in the living room. "Your family, we will all stay a short while longer, then leave you and Shayla. She needs rest so she does not have the baby before the priest blesses your union. As for the preparations for the ceremony, Nonna and I will take care of these."

Draco inclined his head. "*Grazie*. Shayla and I will arrange for a license tomorrow."

Primo proved himself as good as his word. Within the hour, everyone pitched in to sweep the house clean of clutter and debris. Leftover food disappeared into Draco's cavernous refrigerator, neatly wrapped and labeled. Hugs and kisses were freely dispensed. Then, one by one, the Dantes departed.

An abrupt silence crashed down around Draco and Shayla, strumming to life an unexpected awkwardness. "Why don't I show you the house," he suggested in an effort to break the intensity of the moment.

Shayla seized on the suggestion with patent relief. "I'd like that. I feel like I've been sitting forever."

He took her through the house, pleased by her sincere pleasure and delight at the vaulted ceilings, open spaces and endless windows that offered spectacular views of Angel Island, Belvedere and the bay. The instant he realized exhaustion had replaced enjoyment, he urged her upstairs, where he intended to tuck her into bed as soon as possible.

He opened the door to the master bedroom. "You're welcome to join me in here." One look at her face gave him the unwelcome answer to that suggestion. "But perhaps you'd be more comfortable in this room."

He led her past a tightly closed door toward a bedroom at

the far end of the house from the master suite. She paused outside of the middle room. "What's in here?" she asked.

"Another bedroom," he said dismissively. "It doesn't have a private bath, so—" He attempted to urge her past, but she didn't budge from her position.

Pulling free of his arm, she opened the door and stepped inside. Her breath caught. He'd hoped to inspect the room before showing it to Shayla since he'd only given the decorator and his cousin's wife, Ariana, two days to complete it and hadn't been certain whether their efforts had met with success.

Draco entered behind Shayla and discovered that his demands had not just been met, but exceeded. Whimsy ruled. Silly abounded. Wondrous had ventured into the nursery and nestled in to stay. Shayla wandered deeper into the room, touching the lace-edged changing table with its silly mobile hanging above it. Real and imaginary creatures dangled in every imaginable position from the strings. Some clung for dear life, others hung by wings or toes, one by its tail, each with comical expressions.

The walls were the only part of the room left incomplete, he noted, and blessed Ariana for what she'd been able to finish. Three were painted to resemble a magical forest, rife with playful fairies and trolls and other fantastical creatures. Anyone who saw them would instantly identify them as the work of Ariana's alter ego—Mrs. Pennywinkle, children's book author and illustrator. But the one behind the crib remained notably blank.

Oh, well. He'd tried. And he could guarantee that she had, as well. Considering how surprised the family had been by Shayla's pregnancy, it was clear that Ariana had acceded to his wishes and remained mum about his request for a nursery, even from her husband, Lazz. His mouth curved into a wry smile. Though she hadn't warned him about the housewarming party, no doubt her way to balance the scales.

For the rest of the room, Draco had recommended yellow as the overriding color since it echoed one of the blankets Shayla had made for the baby. The crib was simple and sturdy and rated the safest on the market, the rocking chair positioned adjacent to it the most comfortable money could buy. A baby monitor stood at the ready.

She crossed to the dresser and opened a few of the drawers to reveal garments so tiny it made Draco nervous to imagine their having a baby who could fit into them. Last of all, she opened the louvered closet doors to reveal colorful containers overflowing with toys.

He shifted in place. "I might have gotten carried away."

She glanced over her shoulder and lifted an eyebrow. "Might?"

He blew out his breath. "Did." He shot an uneasy glance around the room, striving to see it through Shayla's eyes. "I guess I should have waited so you could have some input."

She turned to regard him through watchful eyes. "How much input did you have? You only found out about my pregnancy, what? Two days ago?"

Was she upset because he hadn't included her in the decision making? He shrugged. "I wish we could have chosen everything ourselves, but I wasn't sure there'd be time before the baby was born." His mouth quirked into a smile. "I did some research and explained to the decorator what I wanted, I gather at greater length and with more detail than any other room in the house. At least, that's what he finally told me."

Shayla approached. To his surprise, she folded her arms around his neck and tugged him down for a slow, sweet kiss. "Thank you. This is amazing. It's also absolutely perfect."

He rested his forehead against hers. "I know you want

your own place. But maybe for the first few months it would work best to stay here where I can help."

She surprised him again by nodding. "That sounds reasonable. I don't have a problem living with you for the time being so long as you stick to our pact and I can move into my own place when I'm ready."

It wasn't a total surrender, but it gave him time. Time to convince her to turn "for the time being" into plain old forever. To create a real marriage together and a real family. Maybe he could prove that he'd never confine her, but would give her the freedom she craved to accomplish new goals. Craft new dreams. Better dreams. Somehow, someway, he needed to provide her with all the things she lacked so she'd stay instead of run.

Slow down, Dante. First things first, and patience would be at the top of his to-do list, even though it was in seriously short supply these days. He inclined his head toward the door. "Why don't I show you your room?" he offered with an easy smile.

He ushered her into the room next to the nursery. It was smaller than his but with a private bath, small sitting area and cantilevered redwood deck that wrapped around the house and connected with his bedroom. He'd considered having a door cut into the nursery so it accessed the deck, as well, but decided against it for safety reasons.

"We can move the crib and rocker in here temporarily if that would be easier for you," he offered.

She nodded and he caught a flash of exhaustion buried in her eyes. "Thank you. I'd prefer that."

He swept back the bedcovers with one hand and gathered her up with the other. "We can decide all that later. Right now, you need sleep. Dr. Dorling would be furious if he knew we hadn't tucked you in the instant we arrived."

He didn't give her a chance to protest, but eased her onto

the mattress. Kneeling, he removed her shoes. "Do you want to strip down or will you be comfortable enough like this?"

"I'm too tired to strip down," she confessed.

"Then sleep. I'll bring the bags up in a little while along with some dinner and you can change then. You can even indulge yourself and eat in bed."

She yawned, half smothering her reply. "After that meal your relatives prepared, I don't think I'll be able to eat again for a week."

He helped settle her in bed and arranged the pillows for added comfort and support. "Some soup, then?"

Shayla's eyes drooped and she sighed in pleasure. "Some of that minestrone your grandfather made? I've never tasted anything so delicious."

"Absolutely."

He doubted she heard his response. She fell sound asleep on her last word. He checked on her periodically, not the least surprised when she didn't stir. Long after the sun set and evening had deepened into night, he slipped into the room once again. It was clear she wouldn't wake until morning and he gently unbuttoned her dress, easing it off. He debated stripping away all her clothing, but decided she might feel self-conscious about his seeing her naked so late in her pregnancy.

Personally, he thought her unbelievably beautiful. She was softer than before, rounder, her curves lush with impending motherhood. There was also an ethereal radiance about her, an otherworldliness that made him hesitant to touch her, as though she'd magically vanish if he dared lay a hand on her. Vanish like one of the mystical creatures decorating the nursery walls. The mere thought of her disappearing again caused his heart to give a painful lurch.

Soon she'd be both wife and mother, just as he'd be husband

and father. How odd that two short days before he'd been neither of those things, hadn't even known that one reckless night with this woman had created a child. But he found himself fiercely glad that it had happened, that a new life had been breathed into existence from a moment of perfect passion.

He knelt beside the bed and rested his hand against the baby Shayla held safely tucked within her. The Inferno hummed as though recognizing its connection to what snuggled beneath. Draco closed his eyes, realizing he'd fallen and fallen hard. For mother. For child. And then he pressed his cheek to that restless mound, whispered to his son and made promises he'd do everything within his power to keep.

Shayla woke with the sun and sighed in pleasure. It had become more and more difficult to find a comfortable position while her pregnancy came closer and closer to term. But somehow, Draco's spare bed offered the sort of support and relaxation she hadn't experienced in months. She stretched, only then discovering the muscular arm cradling her belly, felt the warm male body spooning her own and buttressing her back and legs.

"This is nice. I could get used to this," Draco rumbled sleepily.

"Easy for you to say. You're not currently a blimp." But it *was* nice, Shayla privately conceded. And she could absolutely get used to it. She shot him a wry look over her shoulder. "Just out of curiosity, what are you doing in my bed?"

"Getting acquainted with our son." He nuzzled the curve of her neck with a raspy cheek. "Getting reacquainted with his mother, too."

She took a quick peek beneath the covers, relieved to see that she still wore two scraps of silk and lace, not that they offered much protection considering how thin they were.

Or how they failed to conceal the dramatic changes to her shape. "And—also just out of curiosity—what happened to my clothes?"

"Gone."

"I see that. Did you gone them?"

"Yup. Would have goned the rest of them but I figured you'd be a tad upset."

She smothered a laugh, which faded when she thought of him seeing her asleep and almost naked...and a full thirty-nine weeks pregnant. "I've lost my figure," she informed him self-consciously, just in case he hadn't noticed.

"No, you haven't. It's right here." His fingers splayed across her stomach while satisfaction rippled through his statement. "And it's even more beautiful than before."

Tears pricked her eyes, tears that never seemed far away. "You don't mind?"

He turned her in his arms so they faced each other. Gently he traced the curve of her cheek, then lower to the painful fullness of her breasts, overflowing from the royal blue cups of her bra, then lower still to the swell of her belly. "How can you ask such a thing? Hell, no, I don't mind. You're a goddess."

It was a lie, but one she could live with. She smiled through her tears. "Does that make you a god?"

"Nope. Just a man. A very lucky, very humble man."

Draco lifted onto one elbow and cupped her face. Leaning in he kissed her wide-awake and she discovered another delightful fact about him. Her husband-to-be was very thorough in the morning. Very. Thorough.

With a reluctant groan, he pulled back. "Hungry? For food, I mean."

"Starving." And not just for food. She eyed him hopefully. "I vaguely remember you saying something about minestrone soup. I don't suppose the offer still stands?"

He grinned. "For breakfast?"

"Why not?" she asked with a shrug. "It's healthier than pickles and ice cream."

A chuckle broke free. "You've been craving pickles and ice cream?"

"No, but I could have," she explained with the sweeping logic of late pregnancy. "Instead it's Primo's minestrone soup."

"He'll be thrilled to hear it. Would you like it served in bed?"

She considered, then made a face and shook her head. "No, thanks. I'll come down right after I shower and dress."

Draco's expression turned wicked. "Need help?"

"I think I can manage," she replied drily.

He levered himself out of bed with an ease Shayla could only envy. These days she felt like an upended turtle, rolling around on its shell. Without her saying a word, he gave her a hand, helping to free her from the nest of mattress, covers and pillows. And he accomplished it with an innate courtesy, as though he'd done the same thing every day for the past half-dozen months. She realized then that his gallantry came naturally, without conscious thought or premeditated intent. It was just who he was.

"You know, you might want to shower in the master suite," he suggested. "The one in here is a combination shower/tub and might be more difficult for you right now. Mine is a free-standing shower. There should be towels in the closet in my bathroom. Give a shout if they're not there. In the meantime, I'll head down and start the soup."

She simply stared at him, helplessly, hopelessly, impossibly drawn to him. But not in love. No, definitely not that. Falling in love would be foolish. It would be dangerous. Worst of all, it would steal away her one shot at freedom. So, why did her heart stutter and pitch at the thought of walking away from him?

"What?" he demanded in response to the look.

She shook her head, ending the moment. "Nothing." She smiled at him, allowing her gratitude to show. "I mean, thank you. I appreciate the offer."

But it wasn't nothing. All the while she stood beneath the soothing spray of the shower she tried to convince herself that their marriage pact would work. She'd stay with him in this beautiful home for the first several weeks after the baby was born—though she wouldn't share a bed with him again. It was too dangerous a risk. She'd put a swift stop to that right now before she grew too attached to having him beside her. Then once she got the hang of being a mother, she'd insist on finding her own place. She'd regain her independence. She'd be free, or at least as free as she could get with the weighty responsibilities of a newborn.

But even as she set new goals for herself and created new dreams she knew deep in her heart that she'd never be free. She and Draco were bound, tied tightly together by the baby she carried. She'd tried running once, telling herself she was chasing her dream. In the end she'd been caught. Fettered tight. And she doubted she'd escape again.

The thought filled her with panic, which receded over the next several hours, though never quite vanished as it continued to disturb the even tenor of her thoughts. While she ate, Draco finalized the details to obtain their marriage license.

"Four weeks for an appointment, my Aunt Fanny," he grumbled.

"We have to wait four weeks?" Shayla asked in alarm.

"I had to pull a few strings, call in several favors, but we can get it done this afternoon." He checked his watch. "That should allow us to fit in your doctor's appointment and lunch beforehand."

She didn't bother to conceal her relief. "Oh. Oh, well, all right, then. You had me worried there."

"You were worried?" he shot back. "I had images of dragging you to Vegas and having you gasp out your 'I dos' while I timed your labor pains."

She grinned. "That would have been quite a story to tell our son." She groaned. "See? I did it again."

Draco leaned a hip against the counter while mainlining caffeine in the form of a very fine Costa Rican coffee. "Dr. Dorling didn't mention whether or not it was a boy? I'd have thought he could have told by the ultrasound."

"I didn't want to know." She patted her belly. "Everything else about this baby has been a surprise. I figured that should be, too."

"Oh, we'll be surprised, all right. If it's a girl, we'll all be downright shocked."

"Is it really that unusual?"

Draco shrugged. "Nonna has the eye, and she said only one girl among this newest generation. Ariana and Lazz already have a lock on that. Their daughter, Amata, was born three months ago."

"Oh, I remember her." Shayla grinned in delight. "She was the one with all the ringlets."

"That's our Amata." He checked his watch. "We'd better get going. We have a busy day ahead of us."

Their first stop was the doctor's office. Both she and Draco instantly took to the new obstetrician, a friendly, outgoing woman who warned them that, based on her examination, Shayla could go into labor at any time. Before they left the office, Dr. Henderly gave them a checklist of items to deal with in preparation for an early delivery. It covered everything from obtaining a car seat suitable for a newborn to preregistering at the hospital.

Since they had a couple of hours to spare, they worked their way through the list before collapsing at a restaurant near the courthouse. While they waited for their meal, Draco pulled Shayla's feet onto his lap. Beneath the linen tablecloth and hidden from the view of the other diners, he gave her a bone-melting massage from calf to toe. Her luncheon massage was followed by a pleasantly quick stop at the registrar's office, where they obtained a marriage license. Then, exhausted, Shayla slept the entire drive home. The instant they arrived at the house, Draco insisted she rest, much to her displeasure.

"I rested in the car," she protested. "And I'm tired of being treated like an invalid."

"Primo called," he explained as he corralled her up the steps. "My grandfather never ceases to amaze with the amount of pull he possesses. He's arranged for a priest to perform the marriage ceremony tonight, at his place, no less."

"So soon?" she made the mistake of asking.

Draco's expression closed over and he retreated behind a cool, polite mask. "Since the doctor suggested you were likely to deliver sooner rather than later, I don't think there's any time to waste. Do you?"

Great. Pregnancy had made her about as tactful as her grandmother. "No, of course not. You're right." Her reassurance only partially mollified him. "What time?"

"Eight. Just before sunset."

It was a sweet gesture on Primo's part. A romantic gesture. "That sounds lovely," she said, then gazed at Draco in distress as a horrifying thought occurred. "I can't take a nap. There's no time. Not if we're getting married tonight."

"Because...?" Impatience rippled through the single word.

"Because I don't have a thing to wear, at least nothing

suitable for a wedding dress." She attempted to push past him toward the stairs. "We have to go back to the city right now so I can find something."

He caught her close and urged her toward her bedroom. "No."

"You don't understand—"

"I do understand, but that doesn't change my answer." Before she could argue further, he lifted a hand to stem the flood. "Don't panic. You're a Dante now. Or will be in a few short hours."

She planted her hands on her hips, or rather, what she could find of her hips, and glared at him. It was either that or cry. "What has my being a Dante got to do with anything?"

He actually had the nerve to laugh at her, sending her temper soaring. "Right, right. Sorry. Forgot you never had the benefit of a big family." He dropped a finger to her lips to hold her silent. "See, this is how it works. I put out the alarm. The phone calls fly and every Dante goes on alert status."

"You're kidding," she said around his finger.

"Not even a little. Since three of my cousins' wives have had babies recently, one of them is bound to own a dress they wore during their pregnancy that you can use for a wedding gown." He replaced his finger with his mouth, stealing a swift, blistering kiss. "Just one phone call and I guarantee, suitable attire will be waiting for you at Primo's in time for the ceremony."

She had her doubts, but they were swiftly laid to rest the instant she arrived at Primo and Nonna's. The women all descended on her and swept her off to one of the bedrooms, where a gown hung from the closet door. One glance warned it wasn't borrowed, but a maternity wedding gown that had been newly purchased for her benefit.

She stood and stared at the gown in disbelief. This time she didn't even try to hold back the tears. The off-the-shoulder sleeves were wisps of puckered ivory tulle, framing a softly ruched bodice. From beneath the pearl-seeded bodice flowed a series of chiffon pleats that would drape loosely over her abdomen. A veil hung nearby, stealing Shayla's breath. Tiny fire diamonds and seed pearls created a delicate tiara complete with a flowing cascade of tulle veiling. It was a beautifully preserved piece.

Shayla touched the veil with trembling fingers. "It's the most gorgeous thing I've ever seen."

Draco's mother, Elia, embraced her. "I wore it at my wedding. It pleases me to have you wear it at yours."

Next on the agenda was hair and makeup. Laughter abounded and Shayla allowed herself to drift along on a current of pleasure, refusing to consider the ramifications of her marriage to Draco—what it meant and how it promised to change her life. She sat patiently beneath the ministrations of the Dante women, Gianna wielding a curling iron, Larkin and Téa taking turns with the makeup case. Once everyone was satisfied, they all stepped back so Shayla could see the results.

"Oh," she murmured. "You've made me beautiful."

"No crying," Gianna warned. "You'll ruin everyone's hard work."

Larkin and Téa had employed subtlety when it came to the makeup, emphasizing the high arch of Shayla's cheekbones and giving depth and definition to her dark eyes. Her mouth appeared softer, rosier and just-kissed moist. Gianna had also worked magic, pulling Shayla's hair away from her face and coaxing the sheet of ebony into a cascade of soft curls.

"Now it is my turn," Nonna announced. Carefully she studded the curls with jasmine blossoms, their sweet scent filling the air.

Shayla stroked one of the ivory petals. "They're absolutely lovely."

"They are from Primo's garden," Nonna explained. "He picked them himself. He thought it might remind you of home."

And it did. Jasmine bloomed yearly in the ruins of her grandmother's garden, its heady scent a welcome advent each May. Elia signaled that the time to dress had arrived. It didn't take long, not with so many women helping. Though Shayla didn't have a hope of disguising her pregnancy, the drapes and folds floated around her, making it far less obvious. Next came the veil. Elia did the honors there. The final touch came when Gianna handed Shayla a bouquet of trailing jasmine to match the flowers in her hair.

Gianna stepped back with a trembling smile. "The veil is something old and borrowed. The dress something new," she explained. She indicated the ribbon they'd used to tie the bouquet together. "And there's your something blue."

Finding herself unable to utter a word, Shayla hugged her sister-to-be, then Elia and Nonna. Three generations of Dante women and soon she'd be one of them. "Thank you so much," she finally managed to say. Her gaze swept the other women in the room. "Thank you all."

From that moment forward the evening passed in a haze. She joined Draco in front of the priest in a garden filled with beds of colorful flowers and overflowing with the warmth of family. Just as the last ray of sunshine touched the gathering in a golden benediction, the priest pronounced them husband and wife.

Draco lifted the single layer of tulle away from her eyes and mouth and cupped her face in a gesture as endearing as it was familiar. "My wife," he announced, his words ripe with possession and stamped with satisfaction.

And then he kissed her. The kiss stripped away nerves and hesitation, crashed through barriers and conflict. In its place it gave hope. Passion. More than that, it offered a promise fraught with possibility.

If only…came the stray notion as resistance slipped away and she succumbed to the embrace. If only this were real. If only they were in love. If only the baby kicking impatiently for freedom weren't responsible for their marriage.

If only they loved each other.

No sooner had the thought been born, than the first star fired to life in the velvety sky overhead. It glittered bright and steady in the heavens, then flashed like the heart of a fire diamond. The Inferno burned within her palm, as though in confirmation, as though it were somehow connected to the star.

A first wish made…

…a first wish granted.

Seven

She was his.

His wife. His woman. His Inferno mate. And soon she would be the mother of his child.

He kissed his wife for the first time, while fading sunlight haloed her. When he lifted his head to gaze down at his bride, the sun had set and the glow of torchlight gave her a wild, mysterious beauty. Eyes deep with endless hope gleamed up at him. And yet the kiss they'd shared, one meant to seal the vows they'd just committed to, felt like far more than mere hope. It felt like a wish. A promise. A door opening toward possibility.

Her arms slid from around his neck until her palms rested against his chest. She stared at the ring he'd put on her finger, no doubt getting her first good look at it. It was one of the Eternity wedding sets showcased at that long-ago reception where they'd originally met.

The central fire diamond was from a Dante mine, and in

Draco's opinion, one of the finest he'd ever seen, equal if not superior to the ones he'd lost. He'd had the smaller diamonds on either side replaced with Charleston fire diamonds as a symbolic bonding of the two families. He didn't doubt she'd catch the significance.

"The Eternity rings all have names, don't they?" she murmured, and glanced up, pinning him with darkness. "What's this one called?"

"Eternally Bound."

A troubled frown touched her brow. "Is that what we are? Eternally bound?"

"If you believe in the legend of The Inferno, yes."

"And if I don't?" A touch of urgency underscored the question. Or maybe it was panic. "What then?"

He tucked a curl behind her ear, keeping his voice low and reassuring, as though soothing a wild creature who'd just discovered itself snared by a hunter. "Then it's just a legend, and just a ring."

"But it's a legend you believe in, isn't it?" she insisted. "A ring that *does* bind us from this point forward."

He'd made two vows to Shayla since he'd found her, heavy with his child. With the first he'd promised to set her free, while the one made only moments ago committed him to love and protect her for the rest of their lives. Somehow, someway, he'd honor both, no matter how difficult. Even though she was right about his wanting to bind her to him in every way possible, he wouldn't hold back what struggled so desperately for release.

The words came with difficulty, but he forced himself to speak them. "What I do or don't believe doesn't change our pact. Once the baby is born and you have time to adjust to motherhood and your transition from Atlanta, you can decide how you want your future to go from there. I won't interfere with that."

He'd opened the door to freedom. Now it was up to her whether she stepped through it, or realized that she was just as free if she chose to stay. She gave a quick nod and a slow smile. Then she gathered his face in her soft hands in a gesture that duplicated their first kiss as husband and wife. And she kissed him with such sweetness that it almost brought him to his knees.

His relatives looked on with broad grins and Draco couldn't help but wonder how long those grins would last if they knew that just minutes after making his vows, he'd promised his wife he'd let her go. He returned the kiss, tamping down on the temptation to pull her closer and kiss her with the sort of passion that had gotten them into their current predicament. If she resisted, it would upset his family and embarrass them both. And if she responded he'd never know if it was because of their audience or because she wanted him.

With a breathless laugh, she stepped back. Before he could catch her again, she disappeared into the clutches of his family and he was forced to let her go. *Relax, Dante.* In a few hours they'd return home and he'd once again hold her while she slept. He could wait until then.

He blew out a sigh. Maybe.

Someone turned on music, filling the air with a weeping aria. Draco headed over to a tub of ice beside a table groaning with food and helped himself to one of Primo's stash of homemade beer. Popping the cap, he glanced around the yard, impressed. He didn't know how his family had pulled together the wedding so quickly, especially on the heels of his housewarming party, but it couldn't have been more beautiful if they'd planned it for months.

An evening breeze poured off the water and kept the temperatures moderate, even a little on the cool side. But all the bodies and movement and activity staved off the chill. He caught sight of Shayla with his sister, Gianna. The two had clearly hit it off. And he noticed that Téa and Larkin joined their small group in the sort of female-bonding ceremony that left him both perplexed and vaguely alarmed. Larkin's head bent close to Shayla's, creating a striking contrast of icy pale against dusky richness, and it suddenly occurred to him that each of the women in the group had been at the same Eternity reception nine months ago. Had they met, even casually? Did they remember one another, if only on some subconscious level? Were they even now comparing notes and making the connection?

Before he could consider the potential ramifications of that bit of speculation, Rafe clapped a hand on his shoulder. "Odd to think that we both met our Inferno brides the same night," he said, his comment an eerie echo of Draco's thoughts from only a few minutes before. Rafe's gaze fixed on Larkin, brimming with the strength of his love. "Or that you were the one responsible for bringing us together."

Draco shrugged. "You were drawn to her long before I arranged that little run-in."

"But I might not have acted on it if you hadn't suggested I fake The Inferno by hiring her as my soul mate." Rafe turned to him. "Seriously, bro, I owe you for that."

"Good. I like having people in my debt."

Rafe chuckled. "Then I'll offer this small piece of advice to help settle my debt. Give Shayla time to adjust. Just be patient and let The Inferno work its magic on her."

Draco tilted his head to one side in consideration, before shaking his head. "Nope. Already came to that conclusion on my own, so you still owe me."

Rafe's eyebrows shot up. "I thought you didn't believe in The Inferno."

"I didn't." Draco's focus returned to his wife. "Until Shayla." And with that he walked away from his brother and toward his future.

The women made room for him when he approached, allowing him to settle in beside his wife and tuck her close. Gradually their circle widened and the two newlyweds sat together for a long time listening while the various Dante relatives told stories, each attempting to top the other. Many of them involved The Inferno and how they met their Inferno mates.

"Did none of you believe in The Inferno? Did you all resist it?" Shayla asked in amazement.

"Primo believed," Rafe conceded. "And Marco. That's about it."

"You forgot Draco. He believed, too," Shayla insisted. "When we first touched and I asked him what he'd done to me he said he'd Infernoed me."

"Draco?" Gianna scoffed. "He's always been a total skeptic. In fact, the night you two met he tried to help Rafe avoid everyone's matchmaking attempts by pretending to experience The Inferno with—" Her eyes widened in alarm the instant she realized how her tongue had gotten away from her. She carefully set her wineglass on the table beside her chair and pushed it well out of reach. Then her gaze shot first to her parents, then to her grandparents. She smiled weakly. "That is… I mean…"

"We know what you mean," her father replied in a crisp voice. "Fortunately, it worked out for all involved."

Rafe shot his sister a grim look. "Nice going, *chiacchierona.*"

"I am *not* a chatterbox."

Primo put an end to the imminent sibling spat by holding up his bottle of beer. "*Salute!* To Shayla and *l'istigatore. Cento anni di salute e felicità.*" A hundred years of health and happiness. "And now it is my turn to tell the story of how my beloved Nonna and I became Inferno-struck."

Everyone settled back in their chairs while the family

patriarch offered up the familiar and the bittersweet, a tale of the long-ago time when he and Nonna had first set eyes on one another. Those born to the Dante name had heard it chronicled many times before, but welcomed the retelling for the benefit of the newer additions to the family who hadn't heard the story.

"I had just returned from Florence after completing my studies in jewelry design and manufacturing," he began, patting his pockets for his cigar. At Nonna's narrow-eyed look, he sighed with regret and reached instead for his bottle of homemade beer. Decades worth of memories haunted his striking gold eyes.

"That night was the engagement party for *mio amico*. No," he hastened to correct. "Not just my friend. My *best* friend. Tito stood tall and proud beneath a stand of orange trees. It was June and the blossoms were at their peak, early bloomers dusting the ground like snowflakes while those still clinging to the trees filled the air with such a fragrance…"

Primo shook his head, immersed in events long gone, his gaze steeped in nostalgia. "Never have I smelled anything sweeter." He focused on Nonna, still partially enmeshed in the past, his expression overflowing with nearly sixty years of passion. "Never have I seen anyone more beautiful. My sweet Nonna was all of eighteen to my twenty, orange blossoms clinging to her hair like tiny white stars. And that hair." He put a hand to his chest and gusted out a deep sigh. "I swear it must have been every shade of brown one could imagine. The little ringlets, they tumbled down her back all the way to the tiniest waist I have ever seen."

"And you," Nonna replied with loving tartness. "Looking at me like a wolf does a sheep."

"Not a sheep, *bellezza*. A lamb. I took your hand in mine and that is when The Inferno struck." He offered a smile filled with both pleasure and regret. "Our village, it was a small, traditional place where they took a betrothal as seriously as a wedding. I dishonored my family and my best friend by taking what did not belong to me." He lifted a shoulder in a shrug that spoke volumes. "But when The Inferno strikes, there is no option given, no choice but one."

"So, we left," Nonna said, continuing the story, her voice husky with emotion. "Left our friends and our family and sailed on the first boat to America."

"Did you ever make up with your friend?" Shayla couldn't resist asking.

"I did. One year, not so long ago, when Nonna and I were visiting our families, I went to him, hat in hand. Tito actually thanked me, can you believe? He had married another girl from the village, one who adored him and whom he came to love even more than my Nonna." He grinned broadly. "Though how such a thing is possible, I cannot say. And look at us now, eh?"

He flung his arms wide to indicate the four generations present. Children, grandchildren, and now great-grandchildren. "This is the richness and bounty God has granted us. This is how The Inferno rewards us when we are clever enough to follow where it leads."

A shadow drifted across Nonna's expression and Draco suspected it was due to the reminder that her eldest son, Dominic, had chosen a different wife than the one The Inferno selected for him. And though Sev, Nicolò, Marco and Lazz were the products of that union, they were all aware from letters they'd found after their parents' death that Dominic's heart had belonged elsewhere, with a jewelry designer named Cara Moretti.

Unable to bear such sadness at his wedding, Draco gave Nonna a smacking kiss on her cheek and pulled her to her feet. The music had transitioned from arias to a more lively beat and he swung his grandmother into his arms and across the patio. Primo followed suit with Shayla, though at a more sedate pace due to her advanced pregnancy. Soon all the relatives were dancing, bright voices and laughter filling the air. At some point midway through the song his grandparents switched partners so Draco could dance with his wife.

He pulled her close and breathed her in. "If I'd been in Primo's position, I'd have stolen you away, as well."

She wrinkled her nose at him, and teased, "I believe you were in Primo's position and did steal me away. Flew me straight off to your dragon's lair."

He considered. "Your grandmother rather than a fiancé? I suppose you're right." The music washed over and through him. "Now that you've heard all the stories, how do you feel about our family blessing? Or perhaps you consider it a curse."

"Not a curse," she instantly objected. "How could I think that after all those lovely stories?"

"But?"

"But… You don't believe in it, do you?" She searched his face intently. "I mean, really believe in it. It's just convenient to claim because I'm pregnant and it makes our marriage more acceptable to your family, right?"

"You heard them. You saw how they were with each other." His hand tightened on hers, The Inferno throbbing with a passionate beat, singing from one palm to the other. "You feel what I feel. Is this pretense or reality? Will it fade or is it forever?"

A troubled expression edged across her face. "I…I don't know."

He snapped his barriers in place, unwilling to chase her away now that she was finally edging closer—the beauty overcoming her fear of the beast. "Maybe someday you will," he replied lightly.

"You never answered my question," she pointed out. "Do you believe in The Inferno?"

He chose his words with care. "I never did," he admitted. Until he met Shayla.

He didn't give her the opportunity to ask any more questions, but spun her in a dizzying circle that left her breathless and laughing. At the end of the song, he guided her away from his family and toward the gate leading to the driveway.

"Shouldn't we say goodbye?" she asked as he bundled her into the car.

"Eventually they'll notice we're gone," he assured her. "And then they'll all smile knowingly before continuing with the celebration."

It only took a few minutes to make the short drive from Primo's to home. Once there, Draco helped Shayla inside and up the steps. Swinging her into his arms he carried her into his bedroom, with her protesting all the way.

"This is our wedding night," he informed her implacably before setting her on her feet. "We may have an arrangement to live separate lives a month or so from now. But tonight we sleep as husband and wife."

"It's because of The Inferno stories everyone told," she argued. "You're hoping we'll end up like them."

"I think we'll find our own way, either together or apart."

"Regardless of The Inferno?"

He turned her so she faced away from him. "I think we have more important considerations than that damn Inferno." He made short work of the laces holding her dress in place. The bodice sagged and she held it protectively against her breasts. "We have a baby due any day. Why don't we agree to focus on that and let The Inferno take care of itself?"

She turned and he didn't think he'd ever seen a more beautiful sight. Her shoulders and the upper curves of her breasts were bared, the veil she still wore framing them. More than anything he wanted to see her in that veil…and nothing else. He backed her toward the bed until she had no choice but to sit on the edge. Reaching beneath the voluminous skirts of her gown, he removed her shoes, followed by her thigh-high stockings. It amused him to no end to discover that she also wore a pretty little garter decorated in lace, seed pearls and tied with a sassy red bow. She acknowledged his raised eyebrow with a smile every bit as sassy.

Next, he coaxed her out of her gown, leaving her bared to his gaze except for two small scraps of ivory. He waited, waited for the hesitation, for the reluctance for him to proceed any further. But it never came. Taking it as tacit permission, he removed her bra and panties. Then, he rocked back on his heels, studying her with a warm smile.

"You are a picture, *mia adorata*. But I have to say the veil is the perfect touch."

For some reason, either his use of the Italian endearment or his gentle humor, she relaxed. She even managed a flirtatious expression. "Do you want me to wear it to bed?"

The fact that she'd accepted that they would be sleeping together caused something deep and powerful to seize him by the throat. "Not tonight," he replied gruffly.

Draco removed the veil and set it safely aside. Then, one by one he plucked the pearl-tipped pins from her hair so that the curls tumbled down across her shoulders and back. He eased her against the pillows, while gardenia petals scattered across the crisp cotton linens, releasing their sweet scent into the air.

His woman. His wife. Mother of his child. He leaned in and stole a kiss, a soft, easy caress. Then he took another, a more passionate one this time. She returned the first. But she dove into the second, nipping at his lower lip. Tugging at it.

Then her tongue mated with his in a dance he hoped would never end.

Unable to resist, he cupped her breast, tracing the sensitive nipple and swallowing her moan of pleasure. He lowered his head and caressed the tip of one with tongue and teeth, then the other, pleased when they swelled and peaked, signaling the desperate want that flowed through her.

"Draco," she moaned. "We shouldn't."

But he didn't stop, couldn't stop, and her protest drifted into a sigh of pure bliss. Lifting toward his seeking mouth, she offered herself to him. He dined on her as though she were the most succulent of morsels, a banquet of delicious textures and flavors. He found his way to the taut mound of her belly and tickled the baby, getting a rapid series of kicks in response. He drew back in surprise, unable to conceal his delight.

"He's feisty," Draco said.

"You should have seen what happened when I rested my teacup and saucer on my belly. He must have thought it was too hot because he kicked it right off."

Draco covered his child with a widespread hand before kissing his wife again, allowing her to taste his joy. It felt like three hearts linked into one thundering beat. Perhaps they weren't quite in synch. Not yet, anyway. But their rhythm would join together before much longer and the song would be beyond compare.

He deepened their kiss and Shayla shifted beneath him, her breath quickening, filling the air with the sweetest of moans. It wasn't enough, not nearly enough, but he didn't dare make love to her the way he longed to, even though the doctor had given them permission. Despite that, he was determined to make the night as romantic as possible.

Gently, oh, so gently, he cupped the source of her pleasure. He breached the soft folds and scraped his fingers over and in, offering her teasing forays and tempting swirls and dips. She shuddered in reaction and her breath hitched, then gave. With each new touch the breath sobbed from her lungs and she lifted herself toward him, urging him on.

It ended all too soon. She stiffened within his hold and cried out as her release tore through her. Draco gathered her close, just holding her. He felt her tears through his dress shirt and murmured ridiculous reassurances in both English and Italian.

"Shh, now. It's all going to work out."

She opened her eyes, and he could see the dazed satisfaction mingling with her tears. "I didn't think I wanted you to make love to me. But I did. I do. It's just been so long since…" She broke off with a shiver of pleasure.

He couldn't dispute it. In fact, he could tell her right down to the day and hour just how long it had been. But her concession gave him hope. "You're right. It has been a long time. I'm sorry I didn't find you sooner, Shayla."

She relaxed against him and he watched as exhaustion overcame passion and sleep slipped across her face and into her body. No matter how hard she fought to hold it at bay, it waged a war she couldn't win. Little by little it stole the tension from her so she melted into his arms as though she belonged. Which, of course, she did, even if she didn't realize it yet.

Her eyes fluttered open before falling closed again. "Draco?" she murmured.

"I'm right here, sweetheart."

"Don't leave me."

"Never. You might disappear if I do and I don't think I could survive losing you again," he teased, though he could hear an element of raw honesty underscoring the words.

"I don't want to leave you."

He closed his eyes and faced facts. "But you're afraid to

stay. Afraid you'll be trapped in the dragon's lair and never be free again."

She didn't answer.

But then, there *was* no answer, just an undeniable truth that cut him to the very core.

He never knew what woke him. One minute he was sound asleep and the next, painfully alert. He groped for his wife, aware on some level that it was a futile effort. She wasn't in the bed.

He shot upright. "Shayla?" Her name escaped sharp as a report.

"I'm here." He vaguely made out her shape somewhere between the bed and the bathroom. He caught the fear in her voice, a fear mingled with some other emotion. Excitement? "Draco, I think my water just broke."

He shot out of bed and reached her side in two running strides. "Okay, take it easy." He gripped her arms, supporting her. "Aren't we supposed to go to the hospital when that happens?"

"No." She broke off with a quick gasp. "Oh. Oh, my."

He hung on tight, fighting to gather up every ounce of self-control he possessed in order to keep his voice low and even. "Labor pain?"

It took her a full half minute to answer. "Yes."

He debated the safety of releasing her long enough to flip on the overhead light. Decided to chance it. He made it to the door and back in two seconds flat and wrapped a supportive arm around her. "Do you need help dressing?"

She blinked at him in bewilderment. "Why should I get dressed? I just need a nightie."

Maybe labor affected normal brain processes. "You're going to wear a nightie to the hospital?" he questioned with impressive restraint.

She smiled, ridiculously tranquil given the circumstances. "Relax, Draco. It's not like the baby's going to pop out onto the bedroom floor."

Somehow she'd read his mind, considering he'd been thinking just that. He also wanted to believe her, but... "Better safe than sorry. We should go *now*."

"Don't you remember what Dr. Henderly said? We don't leave for the hospital until I'm in active labor." She escaped his grasp and crossed the room. "What I plan to do is go change and then climb back into bed for another hour or two while we time the contractions. Once I'm certain I'm actually in labor, we'll call the doctor."

He vaguely remembered Henderly saying something similar at their appointment—hell, was it only yesterday? He beat back the overwhelming urge to sweep his wife up in his arms and cart her off to the hospital, regardless of protocol. He needed to act, not laze around in bed.

But over the next two hours, that's precisely what they did. Just when he was on the brink of insanity, Shayla agreed to call the doctor and alert her to recent events. He could have roared in relief. Then Shayla proceeded to get up and dress as though it were any other day of the week.

All through the morning he watched his wife like a hawk while going silently mad. Finally, unable to stand it for another second, he slipped out onto the deck—while Shayla mopped a perfectly clean kitchen floor—and called Sev.

He didn't bother with a greeting. "She's in labor and won't go to the hospital," he announced.

"Have you called the doctor?"

"Of course I've called the doctor!" he snapped. "Do you think I'm an imbecile?"

Dead silence met his question, then Sev chuckled. "A subject in need of long and serious debate. But perhaps we should save that for a more convenient time and stick to the issue at hand. How far apart are her contractions?"

"Every twenty minutes or so."

"She's in early labor," Sev explained. Maybe Draco would have taken it better if he hadn't heard the exact same thing from Shayla at least a dozen times over the course of the last several hours. "You never know how long that's going to last with a first baby. When she gets to four or five an hour for a couple hours straight, load her into the car whether she's ready to leave or not."

Finally. An action plan. "Okay. Now you're talking. I can do that."

"So is she vacuuming or dusting?"

Draco shot a hand through his hair, standing it on end. "She's mopping the damn floor! I mean, what's *with* that?"

Sev chuckled. "Yeah, I drew the line when Francesca decided to scrub the bathtub."

"Got it. No bathtubs," he muttered. "I'm telling you, Sev, they need manuals for this stuff. And by that I mean *man-uals*."

"Tell me about it. Francesca was the first to give birth, remember? I didn't have anyone I could call." After filling Draco's head with that horrifying image, Sev added, "Why don't I alert the troops for you?"

He hesitated. "Are they likely to come over?"

"The women will, for sure."

Draco shuddered. Not a chance in hell. "Wait until we leave for the hospital. I'll give you a call on the way and you can send out the alert."

"No problem."

Snapping closed his cell phone, Draco returned inside. He found his wife bent low over the kitchen counter, her hands fisted on the edge in a white-knuckled grip. He instantly came up behind her and rubbed her back, gently talking her through the contraction.

The instant it eased, he asked, "How many is that in the past hour?"

She checked the notebook she'd been using to keep track. "Five."

Son of a bitch! Five? They were at three just a short time ago. What the hell happened to four? At this rate she really would pop their son out onto the floor. Maybe that explained the mopping.

"Time to go," he insisted. "Better to be too early than too late, and with tourists overrunning the city this time of year, traffic is always bad."

To his relief, she didn't argue, though she tested his last shred of sanity by insisting on putting away the various and sundry cleaning products she'd pulled out. The next few hours passed in a haze. He vaguely remembered the drive to the hospital, followed by the check-in procedure. Then a nurse showed up and asked ridiculous questions in order to determine his wife's status. Couldn't she just look at Shayla and see she was in labor? Did they really need to sit there and play twenty thousand questions?

But that wasn't the worst part. Hell, no. The worst part was the endless hours of witnessing Shayla's progression from those early contractions to the ones that had her moaning in agony and clutching his hand in a bone-cracking grip while he watched on, utterly helpless. Of watching the monitors that peaked with each contraction and never came down so that he ended up flat-out lying to her, telling her it had stopped and to rest before the next one hit. By that time she was so far gone, she couldn't even tell the difference between pain and the absence of it. All the while, he told her how and when to breathe, mopped her brow with a damp washcloth and practically drove his fist through her spine because she wanted him to massage her lower back longer and harder.

"Back pain," the nurse murmured sympathetically.

When the doctor finally decided Shayla could start pushing, Draco wanted to fall on his knees and offer hosannas…right up until he saw firsthand the struggle it took her to push something the size of a Hummer through an opening no larger than the eye of a needle. Somehow, though, she did it. And it wasn't a Hummer that slid into the world, but his son who emerged with a squall loud enough to crack plaster.

"Oh, Draco, he's beautiful," Shayla murmured. For some reason, she counted tiny fingers and toes, then counted them again as though she might have gotten it wrong the first time round. "He's the most gorgeous baby in the entire world."

Gently, the nurse transferred the newborn from mother to father, showing Draco how to support a tiny head covered in a tuft of black hair. He stared at his son and felt his heart swell with a love so overpowering, he didn't think he could contain it. His gaze met Shayla's, sharing the moment with her.

His wife. His son.

It didn't matter what it took or what he'd have to do. He'd find a way to keep and protect them, to love and provide for them. He closed his eyes. And, ultimately, he'd set them free.

Draco joined his relatives in the waiting room, endless Dantes overflowing the area. "It's a boy," he announced. "We have a son. Eight pounds, two and a half ounces."

"And the lungs of an opera singer. A miniature *Lucianone*," Rafe joked, using the affectionate name for Pavarotti. "We heard him all the way out here."

Sev approached and slapped Draco on the shoulder. "Congratulations. We're all thrilled for you. With a mother as beautiful as Shayla, you'll be beating the girls off with a stick before you know it."

"Yeah, about that," Draco muttered. He snagged his cousin's shirt and yanked him off to one side where they couldn't be overheard. "There's a problem."

Sev's golden gaze flashed in alarm. "Is something wrong with the baby?"

"I think so." Draco glanced uneasily in the direction of the delivery area. "I think… I think I may have broken him."

Sev blinked. "Broken him. *Broken the baby?*"

"Keep it down, will you?" Draco swallowed—hard—before continuing in a low rush. "When I first found Shayla in Atlanta, I hugged her really tight and the baby kicked, like I'd squeezed him too tight. Then during delivery, she kept begging me to rub her back, you know, as hard as I could." He scrubbed his hands over his face, forcing out his confession. "I think I smushed him."

"Smushed," Sev repeated.

"You heard me," Draco growled. "Shayla kept talking about how beautiful he is. But I gotta tell you, Sev, that baby is the ugliest thing I've ever seen. It's like someone made this beautiful face out of clay and then smacked a fist into it. And…and I think it was *my* fist."

"Smush."

Draco stabbed a finger in his cousin's chest. "Exactly. Smush. I smushed his face either when I hugged her or when I was giving her a back massage. But nobody in the delivery room seemed to notice."

Sev burst out laughing, the sound ringing across the room. Then he locked his arm around Draco's neck and knuckled the top of his head. "Idiot."

Draco fought free, offended. "Why am I an idiot?"

"All babies come out smushed. How great do you think you'd look if you'd just been squeezed out like toothpaste from a tube? Hell, when little Lorenzo was born, he looked like the son of Godzilla. But everything popped back into place after a few weeks. Fortunately for the human race, even when they look like the spawn of Satan, all mothers think their precious newborns are the most beautiful creatures ever born to mankind."

Relief threatened to send Draco to his knees. "So, I didn't…"

"Nope. Now, fair warning… If the kid's seriously ugly after a couple weeks, then you can blame yourself."

Draco felt himself pale.

"Because then you'll know the poor kid takes after you." Sev grinned. "And you have to be the most butt-ugly of all the Dantes."

Eight

As far as Draco was concerned, the next few weeks would have been absolutely perfect if Leticia Charleston hadn't blown into town on her broomstick, accompanied by her flying monkeys—aka her lawyers. Ostensibly, she arrived to sign the final documents selling the Charleston diamond mines to the Dantes, an endless, foot-dragging nine-month process from negotiating the original leasing of the mines to the final sale. At least, that's what she claimed when she landed on their doorstep.

"Would you deny me the opportunity to see my only grandchild now that the Charleston mines are about to become the Dantes?" she demanded. She glared when he hesitated. "Well?"

"I'm thinking."

"Draco?" Shayla's voice came from behind him. "Is that the door?"

He swore beneath his breath. "I've got it."

"Who—" She cradled the baby against her shoulder and peeked around his shoulder. "Grandmother!"

With a long-suffering sigh, Draco stepped back and allowed Leticia across the threshold. "Come on in."

"Gracious as ever," she snapped as she sailed into the house. She paused to study the tiny bundle Shayla held. Something moved across her expression, something that replaced the coldness with an almost human warmth and longing. And then it vanished. "I assume from the excess of blue the poor child is wearing that it's a boy?"

"Yes. We named him Stefano, after Dad, as well as Draco's maternal grandfather."

Leticia's spine snapped to attention. "Your father's name was Stefan, not Stefano."

"But he's named in honor of Dad," Shayla said gently.

Leticia relented enough to peer down at the baby. "He… he looks more like you than Draco. I don't suppose he could be Derek Algier's son?"

Draco saw red. "Son of a—"

Shayla cut him off with a quick shake of her head. "I insisted on a paternity test right after Stefano was born. Even though Draco knows he's the father, I heard there were rumors floating around Europe that Derek and I had an affair and I was pregnant with his child. I wanted the facts set straight for everyone's benefit."

Leticia chewed on that for a long minute. Based on her expression it must have tasted bitter. "How altruistic of you."

"You never give up, do you?" Draco strove to keep calm.

She whipped around. "Would I rather the boy be Derek's? In a heartbeat. You Dantes have stolen everything from me. My business. My son. My granddaughter. Now you've even hijacked the Charleston lineage, stamping your Dante genes into our pool."

"Grandmother!"

"Muddying the waters?" Draco suggested coolly.

"Yes! That's exactly right. It wasn't enough that you killed my only child." It was the most passion he'd ever heard from her, her breath sobbing from her lungs. "Now you've robbed me of my granddaughter and my great-grandson."

"The Dantes aren't responsible for your son's death," Draco stated. "Shayla's parents died in a car wreck."

"Because they'd just found out we were bankrupt, bankrupt because of the Dantes."

"First, the Dantes were only partly responsible for the bankruptcy. Granted, you couldn't compete against our fire diamonds. Not back then. But it was your mines drying up that ultimately ruined your business."

Leticia swept that aside as of no account. "The bottom line is you destroyed my son!"

He wouldn't let her get away with it. "No, Shayla's parents died returning home from a night out celebrating," he corrected. Reluctant compassion flooded through him. "I looked it up, Leticia. I looked it up after I learned that you blamed us for their deaths. I read the newspaper account. It was raining. They'd been drinking and took a cab home because neither were willing to drive."

Leticia's chin quivered. "No. They had nothing to celebrate and every reason to despair."

"He wasn't upset about the bankruptcy. They were celebrating his new job. A job with Dantes' New York office."

Shayla stiffened. "Grandmother, is that true? All this time you told me the Dantes were responsible for my parents' death. But they weren't, were they?"

Her face crumpled. "Yes! It *is* their fault. Stefan would never have gone over to the enemy."

"But he did," Draco replied. "And that's what you can't forgive. His betrayal."

Tears rained unchecked down her cheeks. For the first time since he'd known her, she looked her age. "He'd never have accepted a job with you people if Primo hadn't tempted him."

Despite the "you people" dig, empathy underscored Draco's comments. All things considered, he could afford to be generous. "After your husband died, you hoped Stefan could pick up the reins and run Charlestons. But he wasn't management material anymore than Shayla was. He was a designer. An artist. He didn't have the necessary skills for business." He dared to take her hand in his. "But you did. Why didn't you step in, Leticia? You have everything it takes to go head to head with Dantes. You could have given us a real run for our money."

For an instant, he thought he had her. Then she snatched her hand free and her chin assumed a proud tilt. "That would have been inappropriate for a woman in my position, with my upbringing."

"Why? You expected Shayla to do it. Why not you?"

Her chin quivered ever so slightly. "Times have changed," she whispered. There was a painful honesty underscoring her words. "By the time they did, I was too old to handle the reins."

Before Draco could say anything further, his cell phone buzzed. He checked it swiftly and read the text message from Juice. *Found #5. Come now.* He returned his attention to Leticia, but she'd closed down. Worse, she fixed him with a "the South will rise again!" look of defiance, no doubt because he'd managed to slip beneath her guard.

"I'm sorry, Shayla. I have a meeting I need to take." He shot an uneasy glance in Leticia's direction before returning his attention to his wife. "Will you be all right?"

"Just fine." She smiled brightly. "I can spend the morning with my grandmother and the baby. We'll have tea."

"Hmm. I don't think the baby can handle tea, yet." Or his great-grandmother.

She laughed as he hoped she would. Leticia rolled her eyes. Reluctantly, he gave his wife a swift kiss and left. But he had an itch in the middle of his back, no doubt at the exact spot where Leticia wanted to plant a knife. And he couldn't help but wonder if he was making a terrible mistake by leaving.

"He only seduced you in order to get a better deal on leasing our mines, you know."

"Dante mines," Shayla corrected mildly.

It was an accusation she'd heard more than once. In the beginning, she'd gone for the bait every time. Now she just shrugged it off. Her grandmother didn't understand how it had been the night Shayla and Draco first met. As for which of them seduced the other... There were only two people who knew for certain what went on that night, only two people in the bed where Stefano had been conceived, which meant that only she and her husband knew how and why they'd ended up there. She could state for a fact that it had nothing to do with the Charleston mines or fire diamonds or Dantes, and everything to do with simple, irresistible passion.

"They're not Dante mines, yet. Not until I sign the final papers." Leticia folded her arms across her narrow chest. "Maybe I won't sign. What do you have to say about that?"

"Think of all the money you'll be out if you don't sell. Money that will restore the mansion. Wouldn't you like to see it looking like it did in its heyday?"

"Of course I want to restore my home." She paused, fussed with her collar. "But what's the point?"

"The point?" Shayla dropped a kiss on the top of Stefano's head, feeling a gentle warmth radiating from the baby. She filled her lungs with his distinct baby scent and sighed in pleasure. How had she gotten so lucky? "I don't understand, Grandmother. Why wouldn't you want to restore the mansion?"

"Your father is gone. You're gone. My great-grandson is gone. What's the point of restoring something that will never be used by my family once I'm dead and buried?"

"Oh."

Shayla looked at her grandmother. Really looked this time. Unhappiness glittered in Leticia's striking blue eyes and deepened the lines around her mouth, aging her. She played restlessly with the wedding ring strung on her necklace, the fire diamond winking slyly. Why she refused to wear it on her finger, Shayla had never understood, but then, there was a lot about her grandmother she didn't understand.

She'd never been a particularly cheerful woman, more inclined toward an autocratic nature, which was the exact opposite of how Shayla preferred to live life. But she'd always exuded a fierce determination and purpose. Drive and ambition. Until today.

Understanding slowly dawned. "If you sell the mines," Shayla said slowly, "then your fight with the Dantes will be over. You won't have any new battles, will you? No more dragons to slay."

"What the dickens are you talking about?" Leticia demanded testily. "My fight with them will never be over."

"Even after everything Draco said?"

Her grandmother shot to her feet, fury igniting and driving her to pace the kitchen in her agitation. "You think I believe a word of what that man has to say? A man who only married you to get his hands on the Charleston mines?"

"Now you're not even being logical. How in the world would marrying me help the Dantes get their hands on our mines? Just because I'm married to Draco doesn't mean you're required to sell them to his family."

Before Leticia could respond, Stefano stretched, his little mouth popping open in a wide yawn. His ink-dark eyes fluttered, blinking up at her. Then he grinned, showing off his cute pink gums. Shayla refused to believe it was gas. Her baby saw her, tracked her with his gaze and responded every time he looked at her with that same happy smile. Or at least it started out happy. Then he spat up the little bit of milk she'd coaxed him into swallowing before his nap. His little face puckered and he let out a bellow that threatened to shatter glass.

"Lord have mercy," Leticia said while Shayla mopped him up. "That boy has a set of lungs on him."

"He has from the start." Shayla checked his diaper and stood. "Okay, I think I've found the problem. I'll be right back, Grandmother. Then we'll finish our discussion about the Dantes and our mines."

By the time she returned, though, her grandmother had left. A note sat on the kitchen table: *Must run. Time for my meeting with those vultures.* Shayla shook her head. She had a fair idea how much the Dantes were paying for the Charleston mines and the amount staggered her. Far from being vultures taking advantage of the Charlestons' misfortunes, they'd given her grandmother an excellent price. In fact, it made her uneasy wondering if her marriage to Draco hadn't added a zero or two to the back end of the check. Not that anyone would admit to such a thing.

She'd just finished feeding Stefano, concerned that he continued to fuss on and off while he suckled, when Draco returned from his meeting. She slipped their baby into his carrier. His little eyelids drifted closed and his face, a miniature of his father's, despite what her grandmother claimed, relaxed into sleep, innocence personified. She rested her hand on his head, feeling the same warmth she'd detected earlier. Before she could comment on it, Draco strode into the kitchen.

She caught a fierceness in his expression, a restlessness in his graceful movements. A predator on the hunt, came the nerve-racking thought. His eyes flashed a sharp gold while a ruthless smile slashed across his face.

"We're close this time," he informed her. "Really close."

She stared at him in bewilderment. "Close to what?"

He blinked as though seeing her for the first time. "Close to uncovering the person responsible for stealing our diamonds. Juice thinks he can track the sale back to the source this time."

Her breath caught in disbelief. "Some of your diamonds were *stolen?* How? When? How many?"

He answered her questions in reverse. "Six. Ten years ago. And they weren't exactly stolen. I suppose it would be more accurate to say I was swindled out of them." He reached into his pocket and retrieved a folded piece of diamond parcel paper, marked with a set of numbers. He unfolded it and set the paper on the table, the diamond neatly centered in the middle of the thin blue inner liner. Flame flashed from the center of the stone. "This was one of them."

She leaned in, studying it. "I can tell it's a fire diamond, and a good one, too. It's stunning."

"One of the best to ever be pulled from a Dante mine," he confirmed. "Equal to the ones you showed us."

Her gaze shifted from the stone to her husband. "How were you swindled out of them?"

"I'd just turned twenty. Even then I had an eye for stones. Could tell a fake from the real thing, oftentimes without even using a loupe." He thrust a hand through his hair and his mouth compressed into a hard line. "I was young and cocky and full of myself."

"Not unusual at that age," she offered gently.

"I had the stones out so I could prove just how good I was. I wanted to grade them. See how close I came to the expert assessment."

"With or without permission?" she guessed shrewdly.

His smile of acknowledgment contained a bitter edge. "Without. One of our staff gemologists caught me and demanded that I turn them over so he could check them before I returned them to the vault." Draco shrugged. "So, I did. He examined them at great length before he satisfied himself that I hadn't damaged them or switched them for other, lower-grade diamonds. My mistake was not watching him during his analysis. He returned all six to their containers and told me to put them back. Several months later it was discovered that they'd been exchanged for inferior stones. I was the last one on record for handling them."

"And the gemologist?"

"Long gone." He turned to look at her, his eyes empty of emotion. "I'm not sure anyone really believed me when I told them what happened."

"Oh, Draco, no!"

"I'd always been the troublemaker in the family," he persisted. "If I'd stolen them, the family preferred to turn a blind eye to my shame. If I'd been careless and allowed someone else to take them, then I was a fool. Of course, it didn't help that I had no business sneaking into the vaults in the first place."

"How did you get in?"

Draco shrugged. "I lifted Primo's passkey."

She winced. "Ah. I guess that didn't help matters, either."

"Not at all."

"And you've been searching for them ever since?"

He didn't need to answer. She could see it in his face, a

drive and determination every bit as ingrained as it had been in her grandmother. "There's only one left. But if we trace this latest stone back, I'll have the gemologist."

"Will you be able to prove he's the one who took them?"

"Juice will." Draco's expression hardened, became as ferocious as a dragon who'd just discovered his treasure had been stolen out from under him. "It would probably be best for all concerned if I stay well away from the man until after we've proven his guilt."

Shayla studied the diamond again, wishing she had a pair of tweezers so she could get a better look. "This really is a beautiful stone. What's the clarity?"

"Flawless."

"Really?" she asked, impressed. "Were they all like this one?"

Draco nodded. "All rounds. Ideal cut. All five carats or larger. All fire diamonds."

She'd received enough training to know her way around gemstones, and come close to guessing the value of what he'd lost. "Dear heaven, Draco," she murmured.

"Someone lived in style off them. One appears on the market every couple of years, though it takes several months before we find out about it. By then it's changed hands several times and is being offered as a legitimate sale item. This latest one was dumped within the last six to nine months." He fished a loupe from his pocket, along with a diamond holder. "Would you like to have a look?"

"Thanks, I'd love to." She carefully picked up the stone and studied it. Something about it nagged at her but before she could make the connection, Stefano began to fuss again. She frowned as she folded the diamond back into its paper liner, then lifted the baby from his carrier. "He's been doing this on and off all day."

"Let me take him." Draco eased Stefano into his arms and gave him an expert bounce. "Is he hungry?"

"I just fed him." She ran her hand over his head. The instant she did, her breath caught in her throat. "Oh, God. He's burning up, Draco. Feel him."

Draco's hand joined with hers and tension leaped into the muscles along his jaw. "Call Dr. Henderly." He gave every appearance of calm, except for his eyes. She could see a bone-deep fear lurking in the depths, a fear that warned that she wasn't being a nervous new mother. Something was seriously wrong with their child. "Tell her we're on the way to the emergency room. I'll get the baby strapped into his car seat and pull the car around."

The next several hours took on a nightmarish quality. The wait to see a physician seemed to take forever. Finally Dr. Henderly appeared and the pace kicked into high gear, speeding by so fast that Shayla had trouble keeping up. The medical staff checked Stefano from head to toe, then stuck an IV in his tiny arm while he screamed his objection.

More than anything she wanted to go to him, to hold him and protect him. Instead, she turned into Draco's arms. She could feel his tension and knew he felt every bit as helpless, holding himself in check through sheer raw nerve. The medical personnel ushered them out of the examination room while they ran a series of tests. Having to walk away from her baby was the most difficult thing she'd ever done. If it hadn't been for her husband, she'd have gone insane.

But he held her. Held her and gave her his strength. Murmured encouragement that gave her hope. Kissed her with a bone-deep passion that told her she wasn't alone and never would be. When they arrived at the waiting room, Shayla discovered that Draco had called the family. One by one they filtered into the area, lending their emotional support, wrapping father and mother in a protective cocoon of solidarity.

At long last the doctor joined them. Her brows shot up when dozens of Dante eyes fastened on her, all filled with nervous dread. Draco's hold on Shayla tightened, a stalwart buffer, and she had a crazy image of a ferocious dragon planting himself between her and danger, determined to protect her from whatever came next.

Dr. Henderly shot them an encouraging smile. "It's strep throat. Very rare in babies his age, but we've been seeing a lot of it this month and considering how contagious it is…. Fortunately, you discovered it early, so try not to be too alarmed. We'd like to keep him overnight for observation and to give him fluids and antibiotics." She focused on Shayla and Draco. "The bottom line is, he's going to be fine. Good catch, Mom and Dad."

Shayla wanted to howl like her baby. Tears she'd fought to suppress rained down her cheeks. Beside her, Draco rocked her in place. "Shh. It's okay now. He's safe."

She lifted her head, clinging to Draco while she struggled for sufficient control to address the doctor. "When can we see him?" she asked.

"Just give us a minute to get him up to isolation. He'll have to stay there instead of in the nursery since we can't risk his infecting any of the other babies. I'll send a nurse for you. She'll take you straight to your son."

The instant she left, conversation exploded around Shayla, relief the predominant emotion. All the while, Draco held her and continued to whisper reassurances to her. She'd never have made it through the trauma of the past few hours if it hadn't been for him. He'd been an absolute pillar of strength.

And more, his family had come storming to the rescue, as well. She'd never experienced that before, never had an extended family to help out in her moment of need. Well, other than her grandmother.

She realized something else, too. Something that shocked her to the core. She wanted Draco beside her. Needed him. She tried to picture what would have happened if she'd been living in Atlanta when Stefano became ill. She wrapped her arms around her husband's waist and clung. She'd have managed. For her child, she'd have done whatever it took.

But she'd have done it alone.

Stefano remained in isolation for two endless days before the doctor released him to return home. Though Shayla tried not to fuss throughout the ensuing days and nights, she couldn't seem to help herself, rushing to check on him every time he so much as squeaked. A week after the crisis, Draco caught her hand when she ran upstairs to the nursery for the umpteenth time.

"Enough," he said, steering her into the master bedroom, a room and a bed they'd shared ever since she gave birth to Stefano.

"But I thought I heard—"

"You heard the same thing I did. A baby sighing in his sleep."

"I need to check, Draco."

"Look at me, sweetheart." He waited until her gaze was fixed on his. "Would I willingly allow anything bad to happen to our son? For that matter, would I allow anything bad to happen to you?"

"No. Never."

"Then stop. You've been a bundle of nerves this past week and I won't allow it to continue any longer."

Her eyebrows shot upward. "Won't *allow?*"

He didn't back away from the word. "No. It's not good for you or the baby. Listen to me, Shayla. I grew up with four male cousins and two brothers, not to mention a sister with a tomboy streak a mile wide. Accidents happen. I should know considering I broke my leg falling out of a tree."

"Draco." It clicked then. "The scars on your leg?"

"It was a bad break. It could have turned life-threatening. My parents stood right where we did, terrified, helpless. But afterward they found a way to let go. You can't protect Stefano from every bump and bruise that will come his way. And they will come. Worrying about the what-ifs in life won't help."

"I know, I know. It's just—" She spared a swift glance toward the bedroom door…and Stefano.

"Will you smother him with worry? Will you clip his wings each time he tries to fly?"

His question hit home and hit hard. Take away Stefano's freedom, the way her grandmother had tried to do with her? Never! "It's just that he's so tiny and helpless."

Draco smiled gently. "He'll always seem small and helpless. When he's one and wants to walk without you helping him. When he's three and wants to climb the slide by himself. When he's six and goes off to school without you. When he has his first sleepover with friends. When he goes on his first camping trip. When he leaves for college." Draco gripped her shoulders. "Of course you want to protect him and make sure he takes those steps without putting himself in danger. But you have to let him take them. Do for our son what your grandmother refused to do for you."

She saw it so clearly, understood it so painfully. "You're right." She didn't want him to be. But he was.

"The past is over." Draco gathered her into his arms, his voice lowering. "Focus on right here and now. Stefano is safe and sleeping in his crib, dreaming whatever delightful fantasies babies dream. He saw the doctor only yesterday and she said the infection was gone. Let go now. Take time for yourself."

Time for herself. It sounded wonderful. She released a gusty sigh. "What do you suggest I do with all this time for myself?"

He paused, his gaze filling with unmistakable passion. "Be a wife instead of a mother."

Nine

Shayla knew what Draco wanted. If she were honest with herself, she wanted the same thing every bit as much. Unable to resist, she surrendered to her need. Utterly.

He must have read the hunger in her eyes, the acceptance in the sway of her body. Blatant desire burned in his eyes, fast and desperate. She heard the rumble in his throat, low and powerful, and knew when he made love to her this time it would be unlike any other. And she was right.

A quick tug and he had her. A quick rip and he yanked her blouse open and off her shoulders. Shock held her in place while a liquid heat exploded deep in her belly.

"I want you. Not slow, but fast." He stripped away her bra. "Not gentle, but rough." Her slacks and panties were hauled down her legs. "And hot. And thorough. And all night long."

He swept her up and tossed her onto the bed. She bounced once, naked and tousled and more aroused than she could ever remember being. He peeled off his own clothes, shredded them in his haste, tossed them aside. She couldn't think straight, didn't want to think. Just feel. Yield. Allow herself to spin helpless and free along whatever path he chose to take them.

He was on top of her before she could draw breath, snatching a kiss full of pent-up fire and demand. His mouth devoured her, but she wanted to be devoured. To be taken. To have his hands on her and his body in her and The Inferno burning, burning, burning until there was nothing left of either of them but the fire.

"Do it now," she demanded, practically weeping in her desperation to have him. "I've waited for you. Waited for nearly a year."

"Forty-seven weeks and two days." His eyes glittered down at her like liquid gold. "But not another minute longer."

She parted her legs for him while he gathered up her hips, lifting, opening. Then he mated their bodies in one swift act. She closed around him, wrapped him up with arms and legs, and moved. Oh, how she moved, catching his rhythm and driving him higher and harder.

The blood pounded from head to heart to the very core of her and she trembled, felt the earthquake grab her. Shake her. Grab at him. The scalding, turbulent pressure building with only one place to go. It sent her rocketing to a shimmering, glittering place where stars exploded and the heavens wept. She bowed back, tight, then tighter, while he took her over and over. And she reached, found that unbelievable delight and seized it, knowing all the while that she'd never, ever be able to find it anyplace else but with this man.

Shayla muffled her shriek against his shoulder, clinging to that moment of wonder with all her strength, while Draco followed her up and over, roaring his pleasure. She glided then, slid into the aftershocks that pulsated through her in a glorious, endless stream. It took long, endless moments before she could gather enough breath to speak.

"Now *that's* what I call a hallelujah moment," she informed him in a dreamy voice. "Please tell me you have an entire chorus of them."

He choked on a laugh. "Oh, yeah. All saved up and ready to go."

"How soon?"

"Just let me catch my—"

She rolled over on top of him, captured the last of his words with a demanding kiss. She couldn't seem to help herself. This need, this overpowering want, was still so new to her. She didn't think she'd ever tire of it. But tonight she'd give it her best effort. She trailed downward, exploring freely, delighted with his response to her efforts. Peering up at him, she grinned.

"I see you have the second chorus ready to sing. Why don't you hum a few bars and I'll follow along."

He glanced down. "That isn't a chorus, sweetheart. It's a whole damned symphony. And I plan to have you play every last note."

And she did.

Draco woke in the dark of night, Shayla held safe and secure within his arms. *Great speech, Dante.* No question that his darling wife needed to hear every word of it—the importance of letting go. But the time had come to heed his own advice. He'd held on to Shayla for weeks, finding excuse after excuse to keep her caged, even though he'd filled her cage with every manner of temptation.

How could he demand she allow their son to fly when he kept her wings so carefully clipped?

She stirred in his arms, snuggling closer to his warmth,

and he gritted his teeth. Just the mere idea of losing her, of having her live apart from him, just about gutted him.

He wanted her. Needed her. Adored her. Would move heaven and earth if it meant giving her happiness. He closed his eyes, feeling the unrelenting pull of The Inferno. The last tiny barrier fell.

He loved her, loved her beyond measure.

And because he loved her, he'd set her free.

Shayla awoke to Stefano's predawn squall, signaling his need for breakfast. He'd actually lasted an hour longer than usual. Cautiously, she eased from Draco's embrace, hoping he'd sleep through his son's impatient cries.

Entering the nursery, she lifted Stefano from his crib and nestled him close. She carried him to the rocking chair and gently rocked while he fed. As always, her gaze traveled around the room and she couldn't help but smile. Every time she sat here she saw some new bit of whimsy, either something she'd overlooked until then, or some little detail that Draco had slipped in without her noticing.

She loved these moments with her son. Sweet, fleeting occasions that would be over before she knew it. It gave her time to think. To quiet her thoughts and slow life's rhythm. To enjoy the now and simply feel. And while she sat and rocked, she considered what Draco had told her the night before—the importance of letting go.

It had struck a serious nerve with her, not just because of her son but because of herself. Until last night she'd thought if she were released—let go—it meant she'd be free. Back on that fateful night when she met Draco, she believed that if she fulfilled her obligations to her grandmother, she would take the job with Derek and experience that freedom. And yet... All during those first months overseas, Draco consumed her every waking thought. And as soon as something had gone wrong, where had she gone? Back to her roots. Back to her family ties.

"Back home," she murmured.

She'd never been free of those ties and never would. How foolish to think otherwise. There might be many things about Grandmother Charleston that bothered her. But when push came to shove, that's the person she'd turned to in her moment of crisis. And she realized something else, as well. It would have been Draco if she hadn't been told he was already married. Because she was tied to him not just through their child, but with body and heart and soul.

She closed her eyes and faced facts. She didn't want to be free, not if it meant living without Draco. Oh, she could find a certain level of contentment if she lived in some small, cozy apartment with Stefano. But she wouldn't be happy. Because the truth was she loved Draco, loved him beyond measure and for all of time.

She opened her eyes and looked around the nursery he'd created. Thought about all that he'd done over the past two months. Her gaze landed on the bare stretch of wall behind the crib and an idea occurred to her. An idea that might express her heart's desire and prove to Draco that she'd only know true freedom if it was in his arms.

"You heard me, Sev. I want the suite for Shayla and the baby."

"I heard you. I just don't like what I'm hearing. How long will they be staying at the suite?"

"I don't know. As long as it takes."

"Look, whatever you did, just apologize. It's not worth having her move out."

"I didn't do anything," Draco snarled. "And before you ask, no, we're not having marital problems."

"Sounds like marital problems to me. Wives don't just up

and move out of their home and away from their husband without a damn good reason. And they especially don't do it a few short weeks after giving birth. The way I see it, *you* must be the reason."

Draco gritted his teeth. "Look. I made a promise to her when we married, okay? And I intend to keep it no matter how much I'd rather— No matter how much it—" Hurts. Kills him. Rips him to shreds. He closed his eyes and swore. "Can they use the suite while I find them a suitable house or not?"

Sev's sigh came long and rough. "Sure. If there's anything I can do, let me know, will you?"

"You'll be the first one I call."

Shayla rested the phone between shoulder and ear while she wrestled a diaper around Stefano's pumping legs. "Actually, I called to ask for a favor."

"Anything," Ariana answered promptly, her voice carrying a hint of her Italian origins. "Name it and it's yours."

Stefano's onesie came next, something her son was intent on keeping off his little squirming body at all costs. Shayla smothered a laugh as she struggled to dress her son and speak at the same time. "The mural," she managed to say. "You painted it, didn't you? I recognize your style from the Mrs. Pennywinkle books you write and illustrate. It's absolutely stunning and I can't thank you enough for all your hard work."

"It is kind of you to say." Warmth filled Ariana's voice. "When I stepped into my grandmother's shoes, my publisher was not sure readers would enjoy my more whimsical style."

"Personally, I love it. But…I wonder if I could hire you to add to the mural for me as a wedding gift for Draco. I'd like a final scene painted on the wall behind the crib, a personalized scene. With Stefano arriving so soon after the ceremony I never had the opportunity to give him anything."

"This mural, it is for love?" Ariana asked.

Shayla lifted her son off the changing table and carried him to the rocking chair. Collapsing into it, she couldn't help grinning and allowed her happiness to radiate into her voice. "Very much so."

"Then consider it done. Now tell me what you want." When Shayla finished describing her idea, Ariana sighed. "I am so sorry, but I am not the one you need for this project."

Shayla hesitated, fighting to conceal the extent of her disappointment. "Are you sure?"

"Positive. However, I do know someone else who would be the perfect artist. Tell me, have you ever heard of Jacqueline Randell Blackstone?"

"The name sounds familiar...." If only she could remember where she had heard it before.

"Perhaps you would recognize her other name. Jack Rabbitt."

"Jack *Rabbitt?*" Shayla flat-out adored her storybooks. And the glass desktop Jacq had painted for her husband, Mathias, one featuring the fairy-tale creatures from her stories, was downright famous. "You *know* her?"

Ariana laughed. "Know her? She and Mathias will be flying in from Seattle this weekend. They stay with us whenever they visit. We are all the best of friends. I am sure she would be delighted to finish the mural."

It took Shayla a second to control the wobble in her voice and she hugged Stefano close, drawing comfort from his warm little body. "Thank you, Ariana. It would mean the world to me."

"My pleasure. After all, we are family, yes?"

"Why, yes." Now it was her chin wobbling. "Yes, we are." And that said it all.

* * *

Shayla glanced over at her husband and smiled. "So, where are we going?" she asked.

"To Dantes'."

His hands tightened around the steering wheel as he said it and he spared her a swift glance. For some reason that look bothered her. Perhaps it was the tarnish that darkened his hazel-gold eyes. Or the taut set of his mouth and jaw. She couldn't begin to imagine the problem, just that there clearly was one.

"Oh, okay," she replied calmly, deciding to hold fire.

Hadn't she decided to live in the "now"? To not worry about tomorrow, but focus on today? She spared her husband another swift glance. Unfortunately "now" didn't look all that great.

He parked in the underground garage in a spot with his name stenciled on the wall in front of it. After Draco unbuckled Stefano, they crossed to the elevators. Listening to their footsteps echo against the cement brought back vivid memories of the morning after the Eternity reception when she'd made a similar walk in this exact same garage. It also reminded her of the night they'd spent together—the results of which were in the portable car seat Draco carried. For some reason she found the memory disturbing.

"Why are we here?" she couldn't help but ask.

"I want to show you something."

She could tell she wouldn't get more out of him until he was good and ready. They arrived at the bank of elevators and just like the night of the reception, he ushered her into the car and keyed the panel for the penthouse level. And just like the night of the reception, he escorted her to the suite they'd shared nearly a year before. Only this time he didn't carry *her* over the threshold, but their son. How odd to recall

that long-ago self and her plans for the future, a future far
different from the one fate had determined for her.

"Okay, Draco. Enough with the surprises." She folded her
arms across her chest. "I want to know what's going on."

He carefully placed the baby out of harm's way, then
turned to face her. With the windows at his back she didn't
have a hope of reading his expression. "We made a pact
before we married. Do you remember?"

She stiffened. "What are you talking about?"

"You asked for your own place as part of our agreement.
I'm simply fulfilling the terms of that agreement. You can
stay here for the time being while we find you a suitable
house or condo. I have the name of a realtor who'd be happy
to work with us." He shot a hand through his hair, the only
outward sign that he wasn't as cool and collected as his voice
suggested. "Work with *you*," he corrected.

She took a moment to absorb the hit and found she couldn't.
The impact had caught her completely off guard and it hurt.
Dear heaven, but it hurt. Anger came to her rescue. "Let me
get this straight. You want me to move out? You want me
and your son to move out of your home? That's what you're
telling me?"

"No! Yes." He swore in Italian, though she could have
told him that if it was to protect her poor, delicate ears, he
failed miserably. She understood every word. "You asked—
demanded—to have your own place before you'd agree to
marry me. I'm simply giving you what you want."

If only she could see his eyes, read his expression. Taking
matters into her own hands, she circled the couch so the
sunlight struck him in profile. "What about what you want,
Draco?"

"That doesn't matter. It isn't important. You'll be in the
city, nearby. Our son will be where I can see him every
day."

She saw it then. The stoicism. The tamped-down pain. The grit and determination to tough it out. Relief flooded through her. He was honoring his commitment not because he wanted to, but because he'd made a promise. One he took every bit as seriously as their wedding vows.

She smiled, taking a swift, eager step in his direction. "What if I told you I don't want to move? That I want to stay with you. Would you force us to go?"

His mouth opened and closed and he sucked in air as though he'd just taken a hit to the solar plexus. "Force...?"

Before he could say anything else, his cell phone rang. He glanced at it impatiently before swearing again, this time in English. He flipped open the phone and barked into it, "Damn it, Sev, I'm right in the middle of something vital here...." Dead silence, then, "*What?* You must be joking." He froze, his gaze sweeping toward her, pinning her in place. "Are you positive? There's no mistake? No, I guess there wouldn't be. Let me get back to you."

She'd only seen that expression on his face once before, when he'd been talking about the gemologist who'd swindled him. A fierce look, one filled with threat and vengeance and an unholy fury. It had never before been aimed at her.

Until now.

"What's wrong?" she asked uneasily, falling back a step.

He stalked after her. "That was Sev. It would seem that the initial reports about the Charleston mines were inaccurate."

She stared in confusion. "What do you mean? What are you talking about?"

"Your mines, Shayla. Or rather Dante mines now that the final contracts have been signed. They're played out—*still* played out. And I just want to know..." He took another step in her direction, moving with predatory grace. "Were you in on the scam?"

Shayla paled. "Why are you assuming there's some sort of scam?"

"Because there aren't any more diamonds. Just those few Leticia removed and enough others to convince us the mines were viable. The reports claiming otherwise are forgeries. Very clever, very convincing forgeries. But you already know that, don't you?"

She shook her head. "No. No, I didn't know that. How can you even think such a thing?"

"I just want to know if it was a setup right from the start."

Tears glittered in her eyes, turning them to jet. "There was no setup."

"No?" He smiled, a humorless flash of teeth that caused her to fall back another pace. "And yet, you ended up in my bed. Played your role brilliantly, I might add. Your shock and outrage when you discovered I was a Dante. Dropping the information that you had a meeting with my relatives before rushing off, knowing full well I'd crash the party. The stones hidden in your purse—a purse with a broken catch. The list. All tantalizing tidbits meant for me to find. Meant to whet my appetite."

A hint of anger flashed across her expression. "Stop and think, Draco. I was just there for the initial lease negotiations. Why would your name be on my list? Why would I involve you?"

"Because I grade the gemstones. Because I'd be the one who would have pushed to go forward with the lease, and later the sale."

"You're also the one who kept his name out of all the Dante literature, who kept the lowest profile of all."

He waved that aside. "I'm sure you had ways of uncovering

my identity. Granted, the pregnancy probably came as a bit of a shock. But then, why not use that, too?"

She darted toward the carrier and snatched up Stefano. "Don't you dare bring him into this. He's your son! He's an innocent."

"But his mother isn't, is she?" He circled her. "You could have approached me at any point once you realized you were pregnant. But I didn't find out until you were days away from giving birth. Convenient, wouldn't you say?"

"There was nothing convenient about my pregnancy," she snapped.

Not that he paid the least attention. "By the time I discovered your whereabouts there was no time to think. To consider. You knew I'd rush you to the altar in order to give our son the Dante name. And you were right. Our marriage was your safety net. After all, once we bought the mines and discovered it was all an elaborate con job, you and I would be married."

"What difference would that make?" she asked tightly.

"You know damn well that my family would never go after my wife. And they sure as hell wouldn't go after the mother of my son."

It was the last straw. Shayla gently returned Stefano to his carrier. Then she approached, got right up in her husband's face. "I'm going to say this once and only once. I knew nothing about the mines. I'm not interested in the mines. I never have been, nor will I ever be. I don't swindle people, as you damn well should know...or would if you took two minutes to stop and consider the situation logically. If there's a problem, look elsewhere for the cause."

"Even if your grandmother is responsible, how the hell could you not at least have suspected?"

"How about you?" she shot right back. "You've even had

experience being swindled. Or haven't you ever heard the expression, 'fool me once'?"

He winced. "So I should have seen the swindle coming?"

"Yes. At the very least one of you clever Dantes should have suspected my grandmother was up to something and dug in to the possibility. Which, in case it has escaped your notice, is not my job." She drilled her finger into his chest. "It's yours."

"She's *your* grandmother!" How the hell had she managed to shift the dynamics, putting him on the defensive?

"And yet…I'm not the one doing business with her." She unplugged her finger from his chest and aimed it at the door. "I'm done discussing this. You may leave."

"Leave?"

"That's right. You offered me the suite and I'm taking you up on your kind offer. Now go."

"I'm not finished with our discussion."

"Well, I am." She stalked to the door, yanked it open and jerked her head toward the hallway. "You can call tomorrow once you've had time to cool off and smarten up. Until then, I have nothing further to say to you. And FYI, *you* have nothing further to say to *me*. At least, nothing worth listening to."

He visibly considered his options, and she watched, barely clinging to anger over tears, while he weighed the advantage of pursuing a fruitless argument versus gathering more information to damn her with. She saw his decision a second before the tears won out.

"Fine," he announced. "I'll leave. But when I come by, I expect answers. Real answers."

Draco stalked past her and she slammed the door behind him. Then he stood in the plush hallway for a full minute wondering how the hell he'd come to be on the wrong side of the door, feeling as though he'd also been on the wrong side of their argument.

More than anything he wanted to bang on the door and demand she let him in. After all, it was his family's suite. His wife. His child. His life unraveling at the seams. But until he met with Sev and heard the entire story, what would be the point?

Swearing long and bitterly, he left, telling himself he was doing the right thing. They both needed time to cool off and he wanted to get his facts straight before he confronted her again. Of course, when he returned late that afternoon it was to discover that history had repeated itself. Shayla was gone.

And so was his son.

Leticia Charleston greeted her granddaughter with a smile of satisfaction and a snap of tartness. "About time you returned home where you belong. Now make my day and tell me you've left that despicable Dante husband of yours."

Shayla hid her sigh by placing Stefano's carrier on the floor beside her chair and across from the settee where her grandmother sat. Since his belly was full and his diaper pristine, he'd fallen sound asleep. Perfect, considering the upcoming conversation would take a while. A long while.

"Actually, I'm here to discuss something with you, Grandmother."

Leticia sniffed. "I'm not sure I like the sound of that."

"I'm sure you're not going to like the sound of most of what we'll be discussing," Shayla responded smoothly. "I asked Bess to bring in tea and snacks since we're going to be here for the next few hours."

Leticia took immediate umbrage. "That's rather highhanded of you, coming into my house and ordering my housekeeper around."

"You're right." Shayla offered her most sunny smile. "I only get more highhanded from here."

Leticia folded her arms across her chest and fixed her granddaughter with her most intimidating glare. Once upon a time it would have worked like a charm. But not any longer. Any one of the Dantes' glares could easily trump it. Especially Primo's. Though, now that Shayla considered the matter, the one Draco turned on her the previous day had been the most impressive she'd ever seen.

Bess appeared with a loaded tray and set it in front of Shayla before scuttling out again. "Tea?" Shayla offered.

Leticia's mouth fell open at the effrontery of being offered tea as though she were a guest in her own home. After a few seconds her mouth buttoned up tight and her eyes narrowed to calculating slits. Shayla could practically see her weighing and considering, plotting and planning. "I'll take my tea with lemon," she ordered at long last. "One lump of sugar instead of two. I'm cutting back."

"I can understand." Shayla poured and served with the ease of long practice. "You wouldn't want to risk becoming too sweet."

There was stony silence for an endless minute before a sound escaped her grandmother, one Shayla had never heard before. A snort of laughter. Then she tipped her head back and let it rip. When she finally gathered herself again, she took one of the dainty napkins from the tray and dabbed her eyes with it. "Oh, Shayla, you are so good for me. I've missed you."

"I've missed you, too." And surprisingly, she had. She considered how to ask her next question. She could use delicacy and tact, but considering it was her grandmother, decided to go for broke. "Why did you do it?"

To her credit, Leticia didn't feign ignorance. "Oh, honey, you know why."

Shayla leaned back against her chair and sipped her tea while she contemplated her grandmother. "I have to admit...I really don't know. I understand you being angry with the Dantes for contributing to Charlestons going under. I can even understand you blaming the Dantes immediately after Dad's death. But that was more than a decade ago. Why swindle them now, after all this time? You must have been able to put emotion aside and look at the facts logically after so many years?"

Leticia played with the ring on her necklace, her restless movements causing the diamond to flash and burn. "It's a long story."

"I'm not going anywhere."

"No, I suppose you aren't."

And so she told her tale. She even told nearly all of it, and mostly stuck to the truth. When she finished, she regarded Shayla with affectionate relief. "There's only one other thing I'd like to say, though it has nothing to do with—" She waved a dismissive hand to indicate their conversation up to this point. "It's about your father."

Shayla perked up. "Dad?"

"I don't think I ever told you this about Stefan, but he was the kindest man I've ever known. Gentle. Generous. Easygoing." She sighed. "Too easygoing to have successfully run Charlestons. I loved that man to pieces, but he didn't inherit any of my steel. You, on the other hand..." She tilted her head to one side and gave her granddaughter a long, hard look. "I always thought you were just like him. But you aren't, are you? You have his kind nature, but it hides my steel. I'm right, aren't I?"

"Yes." Shayla lowered her voice to a stage whisper. "But do me a favor. Don't tell Draco. I don't think he'd take it well."

Her grandmother actually smiled, a wide, natural smile,

revealing a beauty Shayla had never noticed before. "We'll consider it our secret." She placed her delicate porcelain cup and saucer onto the tray with a gesture of finality. "You're going back to him, aren't you? You and little Stefan are leaving Atlanta and returning to San Francisco."

"Stefano."

Leticia rolled her eyes, but her heart wasn't in it. "He'll always be Stefan to me."

Shayla let it go. "And yes, to answer your question, we're going back. Though where I live depends on any number of factors."

Since the information Leticia had imparted was one of those factors she nodded in understanding. "What do you think your Dantes will do to me?"

Shayla answered with complete honesty. "I don't know. We'll find out when we get there."

"*We?*" Leticia drew back in alarm. "I'm not going to San Francisco."

Shayla fixed her grandmother with a cool, unrelenting stare, leaning on each and every crisply spoken word. "Just so you know, this is where I show some of that spine I inherited. So, yes, you are coming with me. And when you get there, you'll have a lot of explaining to do. You'll manage. You always do."

"But I don't want to."

Ignoring the petulant retort, Shayla stood, pulled her grandmother to her feet and hugged her. To her surprise the hug was returned, long and hard and tight. "*And* when you get there, you're staying. I need my family close by."

"No, I couldn't," she protested. "My home—"

"Is near me and Stefano." Shayla pulled back and grinned at her. "Besides, think of how much it'll annoy Draco."

Leticia hesitated, gave it some thought, then chuckled. "I do believe you just sold me on the idea."

Ten

"What are you doing here, Sev?" Draco demanded, scrubbing sleep from his eyes.

His cousin shoved past him into the suite. "I might ask you the same question. I've been to the house. You weren't there. Your wife wasn't there. Is Stefano with you or her?"

"I don't much care for the way you said 'her,'" Draco growled.

"Too bad. I don't much care for the fact that your wife swindled the Dantes out of millions of dollars."

As though from a distance Draco heard himself roar. Saw his fist fly through the air and connect with Sev's chin. Watched his cousin crash to the floor. He swore, long and loud, more angry with himself than with Sev. "She didn't swindle us."

Sev jiggled his jaw in order to determine whether or not it still worked. Once he satisfied himself on that count, he said, "Well, someone sure as hell did. You gonna hit me again if I get up?"

"That depends. Are you gonna say something I'll have to hit you for?"

Sev climbed to his feet. "Where is she, Draco?"

"Atlanta."

And that's all he knew. While he'd been busy hammering on the suite door late in the afternoon after their fight, Shayla had called the house and left a painfully brief message on the answering machine. "I'm in Atlanta." Her voice had come across cool and remote, the sugar in her Southern accent tart with vinegar. "I'll be in touch soon."

That was it. *Soon.* What the hell did soon mean? Tomorrow? Next week? Next year? When she was eight and a half months pregnant with their next child? He returned to their house in Sausalito, but it took him all of a single hour to realize he couldn't handle living in his own home. Not without Shayla. Not with her ghost and the ghost of his son haunting every damn room.

So he'd thrown some clothes in a duffel and moved back into the suite. Not that this place had been much better, though a good part of a fifth of Scotch had gone a long way toward easing his pain. Or it did until Sev's arrival in the wee hours of the morning.

Draco checked his watch and saw a blurry 10:02 a.m. The hell with it. Considering the night he'd had, ten was the wee hours of the morning for him. And he sure as hell didn't appreciate waking to someone pounding on the door, especially when it was an unwelcome echo to the pounding in his head.

"Atlanta," Sev repeated. "Your wife flies off to Atlanta with your son right after we discover the Charleston mines are depleted and you don't find anything odd about it?"

"Right now the Starship *Enterprise* could have landed in the middle of Union Square and I wouldn't find anything odd about it," he snarled.

"Son of a— You're *drunk!*"

"Not anymore. I'd *like* to be drunk. Right now I'm somewhere between hungover and unconscious. Maybe a couple more shots and I can tip the scales in the appropriate direction."

"Screw that. You need to sober up and deal with this."

"Yeah? Good luck making me."

Draco barely got the words out of his mouth before Sev grabbed him by the shirtfront and wrestled him in the direction of the master suite. Maybe if he hadn't used up what little energy reserves he had landing that punch on Sev he'd have put up a better fight. It wasn't until he found himself on the tile floor of the shower with icy cold water pouring down on him that he fully woke—and awoke with a roar of fury. By the time he dragged his sorry backside out of the stall and into dry clothes, Sev had a steaming cup of coffee ready to go. He shoved it into Draco's hands. To his utter humiliation all he could do was whimper pitifully while he poured the scalding liquid down his throat.

"Some dragon you are," Sev sneered. "You were always the most ferocious when we were kids, the toughest of us. There wasn't any dare you wouldn't take. You weren't afraid of anything, ever. Now look at you."

"Who says I'm afraid?" he shot back, relieved to hear the power return to his voice.

"Then why aren't you fighting for what's yours? Why haven't you flown out to Atlanta and taken back what belongs to you? Or have you given up?"

"Never!"

"Then, damn it, Draco, go get her."

Draco shot his cousin a grim look. "So she can explain about the mines, or because she's my wife?"

Sev shrugged. "Does it really matter? One way or the other this all has to be straightened out."

As much as Draco hated conceding the fact that his cousin was right, he didn't waste any more time. He downed another cup of coffee, along with a half-dozen aspirin, and headed home. Once there, he arranged for one of the Dante jets to be fueled and prepared for takeoff. He didn't bother packing an overnight bag. He didn't intend to be gone that long. Just long enough to retrieve his bride and his son, and possibly take a few shots at the Wicked Witch.

All the while the question nagged at him. Was his wife complicit in the swindle, or another innocent victim of her grandmother? Had she planned all along to return to Atlanta once the Dantes discovered the Charleston mines were depleted? Or was there another explanation for her vanishing act?

Unable to help himself, he stared at the detritus of his wife's presence in his life, the feminine bits and pieces she'd left behind. A bottle of perfume, its familiar fragrance lingering in the air, a fragrance that twined through his senses and elicited memories of their passionate lovemaking. He ran a finger over the jeweled hair clips clustered on the dresser, clips that attempted to confine the mass of her dark hair. Clips that he'd taken great delight in removing so he could watch that glorious length rain down her shoulders and back. He picked up a pair of heels kicked hastily in the direction of the closet and tucked them away. No doubt she hadn't because the baby started fussing and she'd gone running to his rescue.

Draco flinched. *Stefano.* Dear God, how he missed his son. Missed those deep, dark brilliant eyes that were so much like his mother's. Missed that crazy little infant giggle he gave whenever Draco tickled his round little belly. Missed the energetic kick and squeal each time he walked into Stefano's nursery.

Snatching a deep breath, Draco started for the steps, intent on heading to the airport, when something stopped him, turned him in the direction of his son's room. He didn't question, just surrendered to his gut instinct.

He opened the door, wondering what had drawn him here. Everything was in place—more or less. The hamper half-full of discarded baby clothes, the closet slightly ajar, no doubt from the last time he'd pillaged the toy boxes, looking for a new treat for his son. One of the dresser drawers gaped ever so slightly. And the crib… He closed his eyes. The crib, so empty and silent. He gathered himself, started to turn.

And saw it.

The wall behind the crib was no longer empty. At some point during the past twenty-four hours, the mural had been completed. A huge dragon occupied most of the formerly vacant space. Draco stared in amazement. One look and he could tell the creature was meant to be him, or a dragon version of him. Fierce, hazel-gold eyes glittered a warning, one echoed by the intimidating stance and defiant expression on the dragon's face. It said, "I protect all who dwell here."

Curled within his dragon arms was a beautiful princess with flowing hair of richest ebony. A princess whose jet-dark eyes mirrored love and adoration for the creature who held her. A princess who looked exactly like his wife. The dragon's tail wrapped around her, and clinging from his tail was an adorable hatchling. The babe dangled from the very tip by his sharp teeth, a mischievous expression painted across his tiny dragon face.

Stefano.

A memory stirred, something Shayla had said at the suite before they'd been interrupted by the phone call about the mine. He'd just finished offering her the apartment, or a house or a condo, offering her the freedom he'd have given anything to withhold from her. And she'd said… His brow wrinkled in concentration.

She'd said, "What if I told you I don't want to move? That

I want to stay with you. Would you force us to go?" There had been a tremulous smile on her mouth and a look in her eyes....

That's when he knew, knew without hesitation or doubt. And he also knew what he had to do about it.

"What are we all doing here, Draco?" Sev demanded. He poured two cups of coffee before returning to his seat at the Dantes' conference table. He handed one of the cups to his wife and took a long swallow from the other. "You have the entire family gathered and we've been sitting twiddling our thumbs for the past twenty minutes waiting for you to get to it."

As it turned out, Draco hadn't flown to Atlanta as planned. It hadn't been necessary, not with Shayla and Stefano on their way home. Instead, he'd called an emergency meeting of the family. "Then you've answered your own question, haven't you, Sev?" he responded coolly. "You're twiddling your thumbs."

"Listen up, smart guy. I have better things to do with my time—"

"No, you don't." Draco's gaze landed on each of them in turn—brothers, sister, cousins, wives, parents, grandparents, before settling on Primo. "There are a lot of issues to resolve, both old and new. And by God, every last one of them is going to be resolved today."

His brother, Rafe, grinned at his wife, Larkin. "I get chills when he turns all tough and domineering, don't you?"

"Stuff it," Draco snapped, but his smile stole some of the sting from his words. He checked his watch, his cell phone, then shot off a quick text message. Behind him the door opened and Juice stepped in.

"They landed almost an hour ago," he announced in his

rumbling basso profundo voice. "Should be here any minute."

"Thanks," Draco said. "Help yourself to coffee and take a seat wherever you can find one."

"Hey, Juice." Luc greeted his former employee with a huge grin. "What are you doing here?"

The tank-size man swallowed Luc's hand in his. "Have some information your brother would like me to share with you all."

No sooner had he helped himself to coffee than the door opened again. Finally. Finally, she'd arrived. Shayla swept into the conference room, her chin set to combat mode. To Draco's amusement it perfectly matched the tilt of Leticia's chin.

"Welcome home," he murmured for her ears alone. He scooped up his son, who pumped his little legs and burbled in baby pleasure. "I've missed you." His gaze fell on Shayla's grandmother. "Or most of you."

Leticia sniffed, took one of the empty chairs near his and glared at him. "Well? The least you can do is offer me some tea. It's been a long flight and though I may not look it, I'm not a young woman."

"I'll get it," Shayla said.

She hadn't responded to his greeting and he took that to mean there were still a lot of roadblocks between them. Well, he'd see what he could do about knocking a few of them down. As soon as his wife and—heaven help him—grandmother-in-law were seated and supplied with drinks, he began.

"We're going to start with Leticia Charleston, since most of this is her story." He fixed his gaze on her and went straight for the jugular. "You've had it in for the Dantes since day one. I can understand why you blame us for your bankruptcy, although you and I both know the depletion of your mines was the true culprit. But there's more, isn't there? More to your wanting revenge."

She didn't bother arguing the point. She simply inclined her head in agreement and said, "It was because of Dominic Dante."

"Dad?" Sev said, surging to his feet. Anger ripped through that single word and Draco could tell it took every ounce of restraint to keep his cousin from calling Leticia an unforgivable name. Beside him, Primo and Nonna joined hands and shifted closer to one another. "What the hell are you talking about? How could Dad have anything to do with this mess?"

"Sev, please," Francesca murmured, tugging her husband back into his seat. "Let's hear her out."

Leticia waited until the room fell silent again. "He flew out to meet with my husband, oh, decades ago it must have been. But William wouldn't receive him. Told him to go away. He didn't, of course. None of you Dantes ever did what you were told and he was no different."

"Grandmother," Shayla said with a sigh. "You do notice we're a bit outnumbered here. Please try for just a shred of tact."

"Let them do their worst," she snapped. Her eyes swept the assembled group and she returned hostile look for hostile look. "Dominic had the unmitigated gall to approach me. He claimed we stole away one of his top designers, a woman named Cara Moretti. He demanded I return her." Leticia's eyes flashed. "As if she were a piece of furniture or a ring he'd misplaced. I told him to go straight to the devil. If he couldn't keep good help, how was that my problem?"

The name dropped like a stone among the Dantes. "There must be more to the story than that, Leticia," Draco insisted. "You don't swindle an international company out of millions of dollars because of unmitigated gall."

She gave an elegant shrug. "Dominic swore he'd get even with us. I simply laughed at him. Charlestons was in its heyday back then. Our two businesses were locked in fierce competition. Why would I give you Dantes anything or anyone who might tip the scales in your favor?"

"Did you tell your husband about Dominic's demand?" Primo asked heavily.

"Good gracious, no. Why would I do that? William had a hair-trigger temper. I felt it best to simply let the matter rest." She took a dainty sip of her tea, added a second packet of sugar and slowly stirred. "We liked Cara, even though she came to us pregnant and unmarried. She worked for us for a number of years and then moved on."

Nonna pushed back her chair and stood, her face a mask of grief. "I will wait elsewhere," she announced, her accent heavier than Draco had ever heard it. Then it failed her altogether and she switched to Italian. "The baby. He is an innocent. He has no place here. I will take him in the other room with me so this does not touch him."

The instant the door closed behind Nonna and Stefano, Draco demanded, "What happened after that?"

Leticia sighed. "The years slid by and you Dantes grew more powerful, thanks to your lock on the fire diamonds. When you entered the international market, I could see the end, even though William remained blind to it. We struggled on. And then…"

When it was clear her grandmother couldn't go on, Shayla supplied the next piece of information to the group. "Grandpa had his heart attack," she said. "It was fatal."

"Yes," Leticia whispered. "It was right after we discovered the mines were depleted. The discovery came as a terrible shock. I'm sure the news caused his heart to fail. His death, combined with the issue with the mines, threw Charlestons into chaos." She spared Draco a brief look. "I begged my son to take over, but you were correct in your analysis. Stefan didn't possess what it took. He simply didn't have the drive or ambition necessary to run Charlestons. We were teetering on the edge of bankruptcy. If we went under it would all be gone. The business, the beautiful jewelry, the cars and parties and lifestyle. We'd even lose the mansion."

"What did you do?" Draco asked, though he suspected he knew and threw a look of sympathy in Sev's direction.

Her chin wobbled and it took her a moment to continue. "I swallowed my pride and approached Dantes. I had my family to consider, to put ahead of my own dignity or embarrassment." She clenched her fingers around her napkin. "So, I made an appointment with Primo."

"I never met with you, Letty," Primo instantly denied. "You know I would have helped you if I had."

"Perhaps if your son hadn't taken the appointment in your place this would have all gone down far differently." She closed her eyes briefly, aging before their eyes. "But Dominic did take the meeting, claiming it was at your insistence. It must have been just weeks before his death, near the time of my own son's death."

"What happened at the meeting?" Draco asked gently.

Tears trickled down Leticia's cheeks. "I begged for mercy. Begged for time to reorganize. I had the crazy idea that maybe I could turn Charlestons around."

"So you were going to try and run the company, after all?"

Her cup rattled against the saucer. "All right, yes. You were right, Draco. *Again*. I decided to take the reins. But I needed time, time Dominic wouldn't give me. He told me it was because I wouldn't help him with the Moretti matter, even though that was long past. For him, it might as well have been yesterday. He was cruel. Terribly cruel. He laughed at our plight. He said…" She set her tea down on the conference table with such force the porcelain sang in protest and buried her face in her hands. "He said that if I couldn't afford to feed my family that perhaps I should apply for welfare and put Shayla in foster care."

For a proud woman that must have been the ultimate slap in the face. Draco spared his grandfather and his cousins a swift look. They weren't taking the information well. He could see anger and resentment in some faces, a flat-out refusal to accept the story in Marco's. But Primo's expression proved the most telling. Not only did he accept Leticia's version of events, but he also felt compassion for her plight.

Draco pushed on. "I don't understand something, Leticia. Surely my uncle knew that someone at Dantes had hired your son, Stefan, to run the design department at our New York office?"

She lifted her head and fought for control. "I have no idea. If I had learned of my son's defection from Dominic, it would have crushed me. If he'd known, I guarantee he would have rubbed it in my face, so I suspect he hadn't been told at that point. After my meeting with him, I salvaged what I could. Then Stefan was killed and—"

She broke off, but everyone sitting at the table could see the emptiness and despair. And maybe, just maybe, they began to understand why she'd sought revenge.

Shayla broke the silence. "My grandmother's here to return the money you paid for the mines."

Her grandmother released a slow sigh. "I always knew I'd have to."

"You did." Sev drawled out the words, a caustic edge to his voice. "Really."

Leticia shot to her feet. "Don't you dare look at me with your father's eyes, Severo Dante, and presume to know what happened or what I would or would not have done. Of course

I'm returning the money. Taking it was no more than a coup, an act of defiance."

Draco lifted an eyebrow, impressed despite himself. "Like when American Plains Indians would touch their enemy during battle to prove their bravery."

Leticia nodded. "Exactly. I knew you'd eventually realize that the shaft containing the fire diamonds was an aberration. Not that it matters." She swept a hand through the air as though brushing aside a pesky mosquito and resumed her seat. "You'd have discovered soon enough that the sale wasn't even legal. How could it be when I don't own the mines?"

Shocked silence greeted that statement. "If you do not own the mines, then who does?" Primo demanded.

"Shayla does." Draco dropped the information like a stone into a puddle. Varying reactions splashed from face to face, from unholy amusement to stunned disbelief, Shayla's the most stunned of all. He took her hand in his, lending her his strength. And he took heart in the fact that she let him. "Juice?" he prompted.

Juice regarded Shayla with sympathetic kindness. "The minute you married Draco, the mines became yours. You would have been informed as soon as the lawyer notified you." He shot Leticia a look that contained a grudging hint of respect and, possibly, admiration. "Would it be an accurate statement to say you may have been a trifle lax about informing the lawyer of your granddaughter's marriage?"

"Grandmother, is this true?" Shayla whispered. Hurt and confusion vied for supremacy.

"I would have notified him. Eventually." Irritation sounded in Leticia's voice. "Needless to say I wasn't in any great hurry to bother with such a trifling detail when I had more immediate concerns in need of my attention."

Draco shot her an ironic look. "In other words, you didn't want the news to leak too soon or you wouldn't have had the pleasure of watching the ants scurrying around when you kicked over the anthill."

"See? You understand perfectly."

"The scary part is…I do." He allowed honed steel to gather in his words. "But what I find unforgivable is that you kept Shayla and me apart in order to prevent us from marrying. And all to carry on the Charleston name. All so that my wife wouldn't come into her inheritance too soon. If that happened the hand wouldn't have had time to play out, would it?"

A fierceness burned in Leticia's eyes, drying her tears and turning the irises an iridescent blue. "I didn't want you to just lease the mines, but to buy them. To be desperate to buy them. Careless. Hasty in your assessment. To be distracted enough to believe the reports—or rather forgeries—that hit your desk about the viability of the mines."

"I'm curious. How did you manage that?"

Her mouth snapped closed, warning that she'd never reveal the name of those responsible. "Let's just say I still have contacts in the business," she finally told him. "And it worked. The reports reassured you while the suspicion gnawed at you that I might decide to sell the fire diamonds to your competitors—once I'd bled you as dry as possible, of course. It forced you to buy the mines outright, and quickly." She smiled, a cat-dining-on-canary type of smile. "The bottom line is…I finally beat the Dantes. That's all I ever wanted. To win."

Fury exploded over Sev's face and only his grandfather's restraining hand held him in place. "And now?" Primo asked.

She shrugged carelessly. "Now that the game is finished, you can have your precious money back, less a small broker-age fee."

"Grandmother!"

"What? I need a new car. It's not like they're going to miss thirty thousand or so."

"Thirty!" Shayla choked.

"That's quite some car," Draco said.

Leticia lifted an eyebrow. "Darling, I only travel in style."

He let it go and focused on more important matters. "Now for the final piece of business."

Leticia frowned. "I don't know what's left to be said. I've told you everything," she insisted. "At least, everything I intend to."

He didn't argue. He simply held out his hand. "Your wedding ring, please."

For an instant, he thought she'd refuse. Then she slipped the necklace from around her neck and set it gently on the table. The diamond flashed with unmistakable fire.

Beside him, Shayla stiffened, then jerked as understanding struck. "Oh, Grandmother. What have you done?"

Leticia bowed her head. "I'm sorry, sweetheart. I'm so sorry."

Shayla's chin quivered. "I should have made the connection sooner. It's a fire diamond, but it can't possibly be a Charleston stone because ours were only recently discovered." She stared at her grandmother in utter disillusionment. "I always wondered why you stopped wearing Grandpa's ring. It's because it's not his ring. You arranged the theft of Draco's fire diamonds, didn't you?"

"I swear I didn't. Please, Shayla, you must believe me." She reached for her granddaughter's hand, but Shayla pulled back and Leticia's face crumpled. "But I am culpable because I know who stole them. He was a former employee of Charlestons, Clint Bodine, and I'll always regret that I didn't report him to the authorities when he told me what he'd done."

"Why didn't you?" Draco demanded.

Her hands clenched. "Because he gave me one of the fire diamonds he'd taken, already set in that ring."

"It is a wedding ring. Why would he give you a wedding ring, Letty?" Primo interrupted. "What happened to the one William gave you?"

"I sold it," she whispered. "To help pay off our debts. Clint knew what I'd done and gave me this to replace it. I was going to return the diamond, but in the end I didn't. And for that, I'm truly sorry. And ashamed."

What a strange woman. She didn't turn a hair at the idea of swindling Dantes out of millions of dollars. She saw that as justifiable. But keeping a stolen diamond was wrong. Shameful. Draco's eyes narrowed in thought. "You didn't return it because it was your safety net, wasn't it?"

She nodded, exhaustion lining her face. "In case of an emergency." She reached again for Shayla's hand in a gesture part plea, part apology. When Shayla took the offered hand, she closed her eyes in blatant relief. "And I suppose, if I'm being brutally honest, it also provided a reminder of all the Charlestons had been through at the hands of the Dantes."

The meeting broke up then. Primo insisted on speaking to Leticia privately, while the rest of the family went off to discuss what they'd learned. Juice approached Draco on his way out of the room. "I hope I helped, but somehow I suspect I've only made matters worse for your family, especially Sev."

"My cousin and his brothers just need time to come to terms with what they've heard. We'll all help with that." Draco offered his hand. "Thank you again, Juice. As far as we're concerned, you're family and your help is always appreciated."

"Anytime."

The instant the door closed behind Juice, Draco leaned

against the table and studied his wife. She continued to stand with her back to him. If she stood any stiffer he suspected her spine would crack. "Who goes first?" he asked mildly.

Shayla turned, holding her cup and saucer in front of her like a shield. "I'm so sorry, Draco," she said with painful formality. "My grandmother has caused a great deal of damage."

"You're not the one who owes me an apology. In fact, of all the people here, you owe me one least of all," he informed her roughly. His mouth curved into a smile that held only a trace of old bitterness, a bitterness that faded with each passing second. "And somehow I suspect I won't be getting one from Leticia."

Shayla hesitated. "So, what now?"

"First and foremost, you get the apology you deserve." He looked her straight in the eye. "I am so sorry for everything I said yesterday at the suite. I was wrong to suspect you of any involvement in this mess. Dead wrong. It was a knee-jerk reaction based on past experience and a bad one. I should have known better. I should have known *you* better."

He couldn't tell from her expression whether she accepted his apology or not. "How long did it take you to come to that realization?" she asked. She continued to hold her tea in front of her as though desperate to maintain a buffer between them.

Gently, he removed the cup and saucer from her hands and set it aside. "My heart knew the second you slammed the door in my face. It might have taken my head a little longer," he confessed. "But I got there. Eventually."

"You can be unbelievably stubborn." A hint of her grand-mother's tartness slid through the observation. "And now that you know I wasn't trying to swindle you?"

He took a step back and fought to keep his voice even and unemotional. "Now you have a choice," he said carefully.

"I've been in touch with your old boss, Derek Algier. He's a tough man to track down because he's such a recluse, but Juice helped out."

Her eyes widened in surprise. "Derek? Why would you contact him?"

"To see if he needed a translator. I explained your situation. Told him that once Stefano was a little older I would hire a nanny to accompany you abroad while you worked."

"You...you want me to leave?" An odd quality entered her voice, hitched in her throat. "You want a divorce?"

"No!" The word was ripped from him before he could prevent it. He fought to steady it. His hands folded into fists as he struggled for control, struggled to present his case dispassionately. "We made a marriage pact, remember? I'm offering you your freedom, Shayla, just like I promised. Or..."

"Or?"

"There's option number two." No matter how hard he tried to remain detached, a whisper of hope colored his statement.

She must have caught it because she stared, considered, then slowly smiled. "What's option number two?"

"Answer a question first. The mural in Stefano's room." He gazed at her with burning eyes, eyes he suspected reflected the hope in his voice. "Did you mean it?"

She didn't hesitate. "With all my heart."

"Then stay." He went to her, gathered her up and held on so tight that he couldn't tell where he ended and she began. "I love you, Shayla. From the moment you first walked into the Eternity reception no other woman existed but you. I've wanted you since the moment we touched and The Inferno bound us together. I fell in love with you the first time we kissed. I don't think I could stand it if you walked away again."

"Oh, Draco."

She flung her arms around his neck and inhaled him as though his scent was as necessary as the very air she breathed. Then she kissed him, a hard, deep, thorough kiss. He crushed her to him, devouring her, putting every ounce of love and passion, hope and promise, into that one kiss. He ran a hand down her spine so that her curves mated with his angles, a lock to his key. They belonged together, but no matter what it took or how difficult, he'd give her the freedom she craved and the love she deserved.

"Tell me what you need and it's yours," he told her. "I don't want our marriage to trap you. Not ever."

"Our marriage isn't a trap and never could be." She pulled back and cupped his face, tracing his mouth with her thumbs. "I love you, Draco Dante. I've loved you from Inferno to motherhood. And I'll love you from motherhood until you're Primo and I'm Nonna to our great-grandchildren. I don't want to leave. How could I when being bound to you is what set me free?"

He touched her wedding ring. "Eternally Bound?"

Her fingers rested on his so they traced the fire diamonds together. She smiled softly. "I knew it even then, when you told me the meaning of my wedding ring. I was just too afraid to believe. To trust."

"What about our marriage pact?" he asked.

"I suggest we forget all about it."

He shook his head. "Or maybe we just choose to honor a different pact. One we made when I put this ring on your finger."

She closed her eyes, fighting back tears. "I'd like that very much." She hesitated, then rushed to confess, "Maybe this would be a good time to warn you that my grandmother is moving to San Francisco."

"God help us all," he muttered. But he accepted the

inevitable. As much as he might wish it otherwise, Leticia was the last Charleston relative Shayla possessed. He tilted his head to one side. "You know…Dantes is often in need of a translator. Sometimes it requires trips abroad."

She laughed. "Are you asking me to be your wife or trying to get rid of me in the hopes that I'll take my grandmother with me?"

"Tempting. Very tempting." Then he replied, with bone-deep honesty, "I'm trying to make your dreams come true."

She slipped back into his arms and wrapped herself around him. "Stop trying," she whispered against his mouth. "You already have. Now let me take a turn at making yours come true."

"You just did, my love." He held her close and linked his hand with hers, feeling The Inferno well up, solidifying the bond between them. "You just did." Then he lost himself in her kiss. In her embrace.

The dragon had finally found his mate. And as soon as possible he intended to carry her back to his lair and keep her there for a long, long time to come.

* * * * *

There's at least one more Dante story to be told—
Gianna has to find her Inferno mate!

But first check out Day's next title,
CLAIMED: THE PREGNANT HEIRESS—
the first in Desire's TYCOON'S HOMECOMING series!

COMING NEXT MONTH

Available January 11, 2011

SDCNM1210

REQUEST YOUR FREE BOOKS!

2 FREE NOVELS
PLUS 2
FREE GIFTS!

Silhouette

Desire®

Passionate, Powerful, Provocative!

YES! Please send me 2 FREE Silhouette Desire® novels and my 2 FREE gifts (gifts are worth about $10). After receiving them, if I don't wish to receive any more books, I can return the shipping statement marked "cancel." If I don't cancel, I will receive 6 brand-new novels every month and be billed just $4.05 per book in the U.S. or $4.74 per book in Canada. That's a saving of at least 15% off the cover price! It's quite a bargain! Shipping and handling is just 50¢ per book.* I understand that accepting the 2 free books and gifts places me under no obligation to buy anything. I can always return a shipment and cancel at any time. Even if I never buy another book, the two free books and gifts are mine to keep forever.

225/326 SDN E5QG

Name _____ (PLEASE PRINT) _____

Address _____ Apt. #

City _____ State/Prov. _____ Zip/Postal Code

Signature (if under 18, a parent or guardian must sign)

Mail to the Silhouette Reader Service:
IN U.S.A.: P.O. Box 1867, Buffalo, NY 14240-1867
IN CANADA: P.O. Box 609, Fort Erie, Ontario L2A 5X3

Not valid for current subscribers to Silhouette Desire books.

Want to try two free books from another line?
Call 1-800-873-8635 or visit www.morefreebooks.com.

* Terms and prices subject to change without notice. Prices do not include applicable taxes. N.Y. residents add applicable sales tax. Canadian residents will be charged applicable provincial taxes and GST. Offer not valid in Quebec. This offer is limited to one order per household. All orders subject to approval. Credit or debit balances in a customer's account(s) may be offset by any other outstanding balance owed by or to the customer. Please allow 4 to 6 weeks for delivery. Offer available while quantities last.

Your Privacy: Silhouette Books is committed to protecting your privacy. Our Privacy Policy is available online at www.eHarlequin.com or upon request from the Reader Service. From time to time we make our lists of customers available to reputable third parties who may have a product or service of interest to you. If you would prefer we not share your name and address, please check here. ☐

Help us get it right—We strive for accurate, respectful and relevant communications. To clarify or modify your communication preferences, visit us at www.ReaderService.com/consumerchoice.

SDES10R

HARLEQUIN®

A *Romance*

FOR EVERY MOOD™

Spotlight on

Classic

Quintessential, modern love stories
that are romance at its finest.

See the next page
to enjoy a sneak peek from
the Harlequin Presents® series.

*Harlequin Presents® is thrilled
to introduce the first installment of
an epic tale of passion and drama by*
**USA TODAY *Bestselling Author*
Penny Jordan!**

*When buttoned-up Giselle first meets
the devastatingly handsome Saul Parenti,
the heat between them is explosive....*

"LET ME GET THIS STRAIGHT. Are you actually suggesting that I would stoop to that kind of game playing?"

Saul came out from behind his desk and walked toward her. Giselle could smell his hot male scent and it was making her dizzy, igniting a low, dull, pulsing ache that was taking over her whole body.

Giselle defended her suspicions. "You don't want me here."

"No," Saul agreed, "I don't."

And then he did what he had sworn he would not do, cursing himself beneath his breath as he reached for her, pulling her fiercely into his arms and kissing her with all the pent-up fury she had aroused in him from the moment he had first seen her.

Giselle certainly *wanted* to resist him. But the hand she raised to push him away developed a will of its own and was sliding along his bare arm beneath the sleeve of his shirt, and the body that should have been arching away from him was instead melting into him.

Beneath the pressure of his kiss he could feel and taste her gasp of undeniable response to him. He wanted to devour her, take her and drive them both until they were equally satiated—even whilst the anger within him that she should make him feel that way roared and burned its resentment of his need.

She was helpless, Giselle recognized, totally unable to withstand the storm lashing at her, able only to cling to the man who was the cause of it and pray that she would survive.

Somewhere else in the building a door banged. The sound exploded into the sensual tension that had enclosed them, driving them apart. Saul's chest was rising and falling as he fought for control; Giselle's whole body was trembling.

Without a word she turned and ran.

Find out what happens when Saul and Giselle succumb to their irresistible desire in

THE RELUCTANT SURRENDER

Available January 2011 from Harlequin Presents®